"Why Are You Here?" Jo Asked.

"To give you a copy of the script and to do some preliminary rehearsals." Bob pulled the "script" from his back pocket and flipped the pages. "Here." He crowded her backward through the doorway, and closed the door behind them.

"When the curtain opens," Josephine said patiently, "I am in bed. And I stay in bed, asleep, during the entire production."

"Well," he said rather ponderously, "as Papa, I have to check out the house and then get into bed with my 'wife' and we should practice that."

"I don't believe we need to practice."

"What if I pull the covers off you? What if I swat you on your bottom and say, 'It's Christmas, wife! How about a little?' "

She blushed scarlet.

He laughed wickedly. "I need to know exactly how I should do this."

Dear Reader,

Happy holidays! At this busy time of year, I think it's extra important for you to take some time out for yourself. And what better way to get away from all the hustle and bustle of the season than to curl up somewhere with a Silhouette Desire novel? In addition, these books can make great gifts. Celebrate this season by giving the gift of love!

To get yourself in the holiday spirit, you should start with Lass Small's delightful *Man of the Month* book, *'Twas the Night*. Our hero has a plain name— Bob Brown—but as you fans of Lass Small all know, this will be no plain story. It's whimsical fun that only Lass can create.

The rest of December's lineup is equally wonderful. First, popular author Mary Lynn Baxter brings us a sexy, emotional love story, *Marriage, Diamond Style*. This is a book you'll want to keep. Next, Justine Davis makes her Silhouette Desire debut with *Angel for Hire*. The hero of this very special story is a *real* angel. The month is completed with stellar books by Jackie Merritt, Donna Carlisle and Peggy Moreland—winners all!

So go wild with Desire, and have a *wonderful* holiday season.

All the best,

Lucia Macro
Senior Editor

LASS SMALL
'TWAS THE NIGHT

SILHOUETTE *Desire*®

Published by Silhouette Books New York

America's Publisher of Contemporary Romance

SILHOUETTE BOOKS
300 East 42nd St., New York, N.Y. 10017

'TWAS THE NIGHT

ISBN: 0-373-05684-2

First Silhouette Books printing December 1991

Printed in the U.S.A.

Books by Lass Small

Silhouette Desire

Tangled Web #241
To Meet Again #322
Stolen Day #341
Possibles #356
Intrusive Man #373
To Love Again #397
Blindman's Bluff #413
Goldilocks and the Behr #437
Hide and Seek #453
Red Rover #491
Odd Man Out #505
Tagged #534
Contact #548
Wrong Address, Right Place #569
Not Easy #578
The Loner #594
Four Dollars and Fifty-One Cents #613
No Trespassing Allowed #638
The Molly Q #655
'Twas the Night #684

Silhouette Romance

An Irritating Man #444
Snow Bird #521

Silhouette Books

Silhouette Christmas Stories 1989
"Voice of the Turtles"

LASS SMALL

finds living on this planet at this time a fascinating experience. People are amazing. She thinks that to be a teller of tales of people, places and things is absolutely marvelous.

Happy Holidays and an enjoyable new year to all.

One

That summer, Bob Brown returned to his hometown of Temple, just beyond the southern edge of Cleveland, Ohio. He drove slowly along the familiar curbless streets and looked around. The air was hot, the wind lazy and from the southwest. It was August.

Summers in the Midwest weren't for people. The hot and humid weather wasn't good for anything but growing corn, and Bob's parents didn't believe in airconditioning. Disgruntled, Bob idled along through the town toward the Brown house. It was at the south edge of Temple, just that much farther away from Cleveland.

Bob had been reluctant to ask his parents for sanctuary, but the only other choice was to borrow money. That was something forbidden by ingrained Brown family tradition.

However, while they couldn't borrow money, any of the actual or acquired Brown children were always welcome to come home again. It just grated on Bob's pride to have to move back. He was thirty years old, six feet tall with dark hair and blue eyes. He was jobless and broke. Not quite broken, just bent and penniless.

His car rolled slowly to a stop. The limbs of a big elm stretched out over the whole side yard. Besides the tractor resting in the tree's shade, there were various vehicles that were familiar. Two cars were strange. Those cars had to be visitors' because the new foster kids who drifted into their family were always too young to drive.

One car had an Indiana license. Since the other car carried her license plate, Bob recognized that his sister Georgia's pink car had been painted green. She was supposed to be in Indianapolis. Someone had chased her back to Ohio? Bob frowned.

His dad was the first to come out on the porch. Built like a bulldog—all shoulders and no hips—the older man was in shorts and a T-shirt. He was trim and wore a tea towel as an apron. He stood there, noting the packed car and studying his eldest child. "You okay?" Salty called in his rasp of a voice.

His dad had been a twenty-year Navy man. He'd fought in the boxing ring, and he'd been hit in the throat too many times. That had altered his voice.

Bob opened his car door and got out. He replied, "I came home."

"Can't imagine you here with anybody left in Boston needing to be bent, but if you need some help...?"

His father was partial to all the offspring and harbored foster children who'd lived in his family. Bob being their eldest natural child knew that well. He said gruffly through his emotion, "I just need a place to light for a while."

"You got that." His dad's rasping voice was like a balm to Bob.

Bob asked, "Who's the Indiana license?"

"A surprise." Salty grinned and the tanned skin along his eyes crinkled.

"See Georgia got her car painted. She do it?"

"While she could have, she didn't. It was a gift from her beau."

"Beau? She wasn't in Indianapolis long enough to acquire something like a beau, was she?"

"She managed." His dad shook his head a little but the grin held.

Bob stated it. "You like the guy."

"Yeah."

Bob stretched tiredly. "Everybody okay?"

"Got a couple of new ones."

"You'll never run out of kids, will you?"

"Somebody's gotta eat my cooking."

"What's for today?"

"Cucumber soup, cold ham slices, hard rolls, cole-slaw, sliced tomatoes and watermelon."

"God, I've missed being here." Bob was shocked his tongue had said that.

His dad nodded. "We'll be glad to have you around for a while. We need a pitcher."

Bob looked off at the tilted barn, and at the cow by the fence watching them with curiosity, before his gaze went back to his dad. "How's the car business going?"

Salty had a new car dealership there in Temple. "I got some customers' cars that could use a little help, and I pay decent wages to someone as well trained as I trained you.''

Bob stood at the bottom of the steps feeling as if he was nine years old and his dad could solve everything. He found he wanted to be nine again, to put his arms around his dad and lean his head against his dad's stomach and wail out all the terrible emptiness of his own dead heart. It irked Bob to feel that, but he smiled up at the older man.

And Salty commented, ''The warrior come home?''

Bob shook his head slowly once to acknowledge his dad's perfectly targeted bull's-eye. ''Hell. That just about covers how I feel.''

''I've been there a time or two.''

''But you were really in a war. I was just out loose and on my own.''

''That's the hardest part. Don't you know that? In a war, you have all the rest of the guys. By yourself, there's just you.''

Bob couldn't look at his father as he added in some emotion, ''And you, here, just in case.''

The raspy voice responded, ''Don't ever forget that. We're always here.''

Felicia was much younger than his father and she came out of the door in a soft, rather trailing flutter of fine cotton. She saw everything: how tired her son was, his rumpled clothing, unshaven face and weary eyes. ''Thank God you've come home!'' she exclaimed as if she'd been hounding him to do just that.

Bob smiled ruefully and shook his head, meeting his mother on the steps for her tender embrace.

She said in her basso profundo, Tallulah Bankhead voice, ''All is chaos, and Salty is desperate for someone to help at the dealership. You couldn't have cho-

sen a better time to come help out. The cars in for
repairs are driving him crazy. People hold on to them
much too long. Just because they bought them from
Salty—'' her voice vibrated marvelously ''—fifteen
years ago, they think he should see to it that they run
perfectly!''

''And no charge,'' Salty added rather placidly.

Bob commented, ''It's still the same.''

Felicia and Salty had five children of their own. Bob
was the eldest, and the youngest was away at college.
They'd always taken in extra kids. Some had stayed
and been adopted, some had been there only for a haven. They now had six living with them. A sixteen-
year-old boy named Saul, another boy was fifteen, one
eleven, two little girls who were both six, and then
there was the new boy who was twelve.

Salty's rasp informed Bob, ''The new kid'll jar you
a little. He's a challenge.''

''Oh?'' Bob encouraged with some caution as he led
his mother back up the steps and over to one of the
white painted wicker porch chairs.

Salty gave his son a look. ''Name's Teller.''

Bob understood that the plural—kids—had become just one. ''Now, how did he get a name like
that?''

''He doesn't know.'' Salty's look continued to
communicate.

Bob frowned. His dad was giving him a challenge?
He didn't need anyone else's problems. He was home
to lick his own wounds and heal. He had no time or
emotion to spend on somebody else. He rubbed his
face in both his hands then allowed his hands to drop
limp at his sides as he took a deep breath. ''It smells
the same.''

Salty chuckled. "That nanny goat."

"No." Bob's eyes were vulnerable. "It smells like home." He looked at the porch. It needed painting. "I see Abner isn't back on the active list yet?" Their friend had fallen several years ago and the house painting was waiting for him to heal.

"No. But he's been coming by with his boy and eyeing the place. That's encouraging."

"I could paint it."

Felicia chided, "That would offend Abner."

His sister, Georgia, came from inside the house, followed more slowly by a man. Georgia's hair was a trifle untidy and her lips were puffed and red. "Bob!" She flung herself at her big brother and hugged him.

Bob hugged her back but over her shoulder he eyed the following man. They measured each other in a look and smiled a little. Georgia's intended was named Luke.

Gradually, all of the rest of the in-house residents drifted to the porch from various places, and Bob was welcomed by the known family and met the new little girl they called Pansy because of her big eyes.

During those greetings and introductions, Bob listened for the name Teller. Teller wasn't there.

Salty watched his eldest and knew not only his son's buried anguish but noted that Bob looked for the problem child, and Salty's heart lifted a little. His son hadn't been internally killed by all the weight of disasters that had hit all at once. Bob had the space, even now, to be aware of other people.

Just about everyone helped empty Bob's car and carry his stuff up to his old room. That surprised him. "No one bunks here?"

"Age has some clout," Felicia said in her wicked purr. "We keep yours and Georgia's rooms as they were and whoever comes to visit gets to use them. They were the big kids' rooms and it's an honor for the little kids to use them."

Bob almost smiled. But Felicia was putting his clothes away in the same places they'd always been, and he hadn't lived at home in almost twelve years. It touched his heart that she could remember his ways so well.

Most of the family went to the community play that night. Felicia played Raggs's mother in *Raggs to the Rescue*. It was done completely ham-bone and Felicia was brilliant.

His sister, Georgia, was substituting for an ailing twelve-year-old actress. That had startled Bob and he had looked at his sister again to check before he asked, "Twelve?"

It was Luke who'd laughed.

And a changing-pitch-toned, hostile voice had asked, "What's wrong with being twelve?"

Bob had looked around and seen a thundercloud face with hostile blue eyes that seared Bob's ears right off his head. It was Teller who then strode away out of sight.

It was that night at the play that Bob first saw the assistant director who slavishly listened to Felicia's every word and suggestion. Bob's impression was that the female was a dolt. And she was redheaded. Bob had had an aversion to redheads since the second grade, when Trisha Walker had wrestled him to the ground, pinned him, then strutted around and crowed with her hands under her armpits and flapping her elbows. Disgusting.

During the evening, Bob just happened to notice the assistant director had good posture. Then he realized that she had to stand up straight to counter the weight of her breasts. She had a nice chest.

On that very first Sunday, they all went to church. Bob sat at one end of the pew with Georgia and Luke, and he glanced down the string of people to note that Salty and Teller were missing.

They did come in. Both were a little red-faced and not quite tidy, but Salty came into the pew still holding Teller's arm, and they sat down so that Teller was on the aisle.

It had been a while since Bob had been in church. The last time he'd visited there had been about two years before. He sat, not listening, telling God about his disappointments. He needn't have wasted God's time, He already knew them all.

The next time Bob's attention was drawn to Teller was as the preacher said the blessing and came to ''—and give you peace.''

Teller was out of there.

But after that, on Sunday, Teller did come along with the family and sat next to Salty on the aisle, but he'd disappeared each time as the preacher finished the service with, ''—give you peace.''

It was a couple of weeks before Felicia's play had finished its run, and Salty finally allowed Luke and Georgia to be married. All sorts of people from both families came for the wedding and moved into the house and cluttered up the place, making it noisy with laughter and talking.

Bob endured the celebration. He could find nothing wrong with Luke, but he was no longer an advocate of marriage. With seriously narrowed eyes, he'd asked Georgia, "Are you dead sure?"

She had sparkled almost to blinding him and replied, "Yes."

And through the festivities and the turmoil of hilarity, Bob noticed Teller slinking around, staying out of sight, watching. Bob's conscience twinged, making him aware that he would have to do something about the kid. No one else had any time. Teller needed somebody to listen to him. The problem was the work and patience it would take to get the kid to talk. Bob sighed and groaned inwardly. He had no resources left inside him to help other people.

It was at the wedding reception at the Brown house, when the redheaded assistant director gave him some of the enhanced punch, which had punch, that he saw her green eyes. She looked like a witch who could lure men into doing something dangerously rash.

He avoided...whatever her name was. He sure didn't need anything else to complicate his life. He stood around shunning her, not helping her, keeping from glancing at her...whoever she was. He saw that his sister, Carol, and the redhead were together a lot, like old friends. But he didn't ask anyone what her name was. Everyone knew her so well, he found, that nobody called her by name. He knew that she hadn't been one of the Brown foster kids, he would have remembered her.

The rugs were rolled away on the Brown's bare floors and the dancing was hilarious rounds and squares and lines. Old what's-her-name was flinging herself around and the guys were competing for her. There was no accounting for taste. Her red hair was all tangled and she looked like a wanton. Bob ignored her

and her ear-catching laugh. She didn't notice him at
all. Even with him right there in plain sight, she never
glanced his way.

Then Georgia had hit *his* chest with her thrown
bouquet, and automatic reflex had made Bob grab it.
Everybody had laughed, but he'd been appalled. He'd
just spent a year getting free from that exact bond-
age. He wasn't about to start looking for such trouble
again.

He'd stuck the bouquet in the punch bowl and
stalked out of the house to prowl until the incident had
passed and the guests had something else to distract
them. Then he went back inside, waiting enduringly
for her to leave and the evening to end.

Why would her leaving end the evening?

With everyone singing, laughing and talking, Bob
knew he was the only one listening to anyone. His ears
hurt. He hadn't smiled but once or twice. Weddings
weren't funny. They were deadly serious. The guests
didn't appear to realize that.

Finally Luke and Georgia went off on a honeymoon on some boat on Lake Michigan. After a week,
they would go back to Indianapolis. So they left. But
everybody waved them off and went back to party-
ing.

It took a long time for the rest to leave. It was almost four o'clock before the last of them drove away.
Even then, those in-house visitors stood around talking for a time.

Bob went out into the very early summer morning
and listened to the silence, soaking it into his soul.
Slowly he became aware that he was listening to the
migrating birds flying high up in the night sky. It was

then that he saw Teller sitting on one of the gates, watching the night.

Bob observed the kid for a while and witnessed him sigh in long pathos. Bob felt a kindred spirit, but he silently went away and left the boy alone.

With the wedding over, the Brown house had settled down. Reasonably. It seemed to Bob that the current bunch of kids was noisier, happier and laughed more than he ever remembered. But he didn't see anything to be lighthearted about.

He pitched for the ball games, taking Luke's place. The brats complained Bob didn't run fast enough. They told him to get some hustle. They mocked and catcalled. Yeah.

But he ate better. Sleep still came slowly. He strained for the oblivion of Morpheus, to sleep without the frustrations and failures looming like giants he could never hope to best.

He would walk to his dad's car lot and look over the old polluters that still huffed around fouling up the air. And he'd say, "Now, Mrs. Carstairs, you know you ought to get a new car. You can afford one, and winter's coming along. You want something you can rely on."

But Mrs. Carstairs replied, "This one is just fine."

"But look at the gas this guzzles. You're president of The Ladies for the Environment. Since you diligently recycle and watch for pollution, you have to think how much of our resources are used or polluted by these old cars."

"One car, Bob, doesn't ruin the whole state of Ohio." And she patted his cheek.

* * *

Bob told his father, "You need to find a billing firm to handle your bookkeeping. It's a mess."

"Oh?" Salty looked surprised. "Why don't you set it up for us?"

"There's no room."

"Yeah. That is right. Hmm. You know that old building on the corner of Elm and Third? It's empty. How would it do?"

"I'll take a look." And he said with impatience, "Why don't you *give* Mrs. Carstairs a new car? Those ladies are so competitive that then they'd all get rid of those old white elephants."

"Now, that's a thought," Salty said absently. He wasn't really paying any attention. He added, "Teller is a rotten mechanic."

Bob said, "If I find him in some car's innards one more time, I'm going to pop him. I had to redo the entire wiring in Jimmy Gates's truck because Teller was seeing if he could connect six stereo speakers in it."

Salty was interested. "Did he?"

"No. He did not. I've never seen such a rat's nest of wires."

"Well, show him how."

"Just keep him off the lot," Bob demanded. "Let him work on the tractor!"

"Now you have to remember the tractor is off-limits."

"So are the cars down on the lot!" Bob had yelled from the door.

And his dad had smiled.

Bob inspected the building at Elm and Third and found it satisfactory. He got the Brown boys, and they spent a couple of days cleaning the building, cutting away the volunteer growth in the cracks around the foundation and plastering up the cracks.

They painted the wooden trim of the one-story brick building, found the roof was solid, and painted the walls inside. The boys were paid for their labor. And Teller worked well, Bob noticed that especially, but the boy was silent. He had to be shown how to do every-thing. But he did listen, and he learned to handle the tools.

Bob told Salty about that. "He seems willing."

"That's a blessing."

Bob interviewed several women and even a couple of men, to staff the office, but he settled on Mary Swanson, a widow whose children were grown.

And it was then that Salty said, "You've set this up, you do it, you supervise and it's your business. You can run it from anywhere in the country. And I'll sell you the building."

Bob looked at the title and saw the building had been bought just after he'd called Salty and asked to come home.

When Bob moved the office furniture into the building and began to teach Mrs. Swanson the won-ders of computers, townspeople dropped by to say, "Well, this is nice. This is a good old building. What are you doing here?"

Bob was patient and explained. All those people were long-time, family friends. They all meant well.

But as Bob and Mary Swanson became organized, those people came back saying Bob could handle their

billing and bookkeeping. They didn't want to be
bothered.

At first, their customers were only Salty's friends.
There was something to be gained by living where
people knew you. Bob knew that his father had spread
the word, and these friends were seeing to it that Bob
had some business. Bob worked hard to get the pro-
grams instigated and organized. Then he hired one of
the men whom he'd interviewed.

Bob found Mary Swanson took to computers as if
her life had been geared to that first contact. She loved
it. And the man was equally interested. Bob wished
he'd had them around in Boston. Not that they would
have changed anything, it just would have been a
pleasure to have had them in charge of his billing department.

It was one Saturday morning in late September at
breakfast that Felicia said, "Bob, we're putting on the
play of Clement Clarke Moore's poem 'The Night before Christmas.' We need you to play Papa. All you
have to do is check out the kids, the fire, the tree, and
get into bed. You jump up and go to the window and
look out. And then you stand and watch Santa empty
his bag. It's no big deal."

"No."

His mother stared as if he'd grown a second head.

Bob stared stonily back.

"I beg your pardon," she said in the chilling way
she'd used when they were recalcitrant children and
not behaving her way.

But Bob was thirty and he'd learned a thing or two.
He said, "You are pardoned."

She laughed.

That annoyed Bob. He gave her an irritated look before he went on with his breakfast.

"You playing in this play, Felicia?" Salty's rasping voice inquired.

"No, darling. I'm going to direct."

Salty was impressed. He raised his bushy eyebrows as he contemplated the fact and said, "You'll be brilliant."

"Thank you, darling." She gave a small turn of her body and lowered her marvelous eyes in a modest look. Then she raised those big eyes to look at Salty. She stared tellingly and said, "I need Bob to play Papa." Her voice was gentle and the tone was lightened.

The hair on Bob's head and the fine hairs down his back lifted. He moved just a little, but he planted both feet firmly on the floor, his mouth tightened and he slid a hostile, narrow, challenging glance over to his father.

Salty was looking at Felicia with a little mushy smile on his face.

Felicia waited, then even more softly, she said to her husband in a nudge, "I need Bob to play Papa."

Salty nodded.

Bob took some quick breaths. His hand clenched his spoon and his other hand fisted on the table. All his muscles tightened as he waited for his father's command.

There was silence.

Bob flicked a quick glance at his father, and he saw that his parents were exchanging a smile that was so personal and private that he blushed a little to have intruded. While they were distracted, Bob hastily excused himself and left the table and the room—all the while expecting his dad to call for him to wait. He did not.

So Bob escaped out to the leaning barn and went right up the ladder into the new hay piled up in the loft. It was fresh and sweet-smelling. He flung himself down and lay silent and still. Growing up, he'd used the barn for refuge, and there had been times in Boston when he'd yearned to lie up here in the hay and find some semblance of peace.

No one intruded into his sanctuary. All was silent. Then, the person-size door banged open and footsteps rustled across the floor below.

Bob wondered who it was down there. Was it his father come to pin him down about being in the play?

The sound of rattling harness came and with that to screen his movement, Bob turned to peek through the floorboards of the loft. It was the nanny goat tasting the unridable pony's hanging leather harness. Bob smiled. The measured steps of the goat sounded exactly like a person walking in the hay scattered down there on the floor.

Bob watched the goat until it walked over to the door, butted it open and left.

In the loft, Bob turned over onto his back and looked up at the inside of the roof. It was comfortable up there. He was home. Home. Wasn't he a little old to be needing to run home to heal? Yeah. But here he was.

He remembered when he'd climbed up there the first time by himself. He smiled. He remembered when he'd lured Betty Lou Higgins up there. And Salty had come into the barn just like the nanny goat had. And his dad had hummed and moved around. He and Betty Lou had lain up there in the straw, absolutely rigid, expecting to be discovered any minute. Good old Betty Lou. She had five kids and blushed every time she saw Bob. Even now. He smiled. It was very comfortable up there. And he went to sleep.

No one disturbed him. He wakened after lunch was over. Stretching, he was only aware that he felt rested for the first time in . . . how long?

His stomach growled, hungrily, and Bob had to be amazed. How long since he'd been really hungry? His stomach said "now" in a long growl, and Bob laughed.

He started down the ladder and saw Teller watching.

Hostile, Teller asked, "What's so funny?"

"I'm hungry."

"What's funny about that?" The boy frowned furiously.

So Teller had been hungry? "I haven't wanted to eat for a long time."

"But you ate."

And there had been times when Teller had had no food? Bob replied, "Yeah. And I didn't even appreciate it."

Teller didn't say anything.

Bob asked suddenly, "What're you doing home?"

"It's Saturday."

Bob hadn't let any of the days be important enough to label. He'd needed only to get through each one and he'd lost track of them. "What'd you have for lunch?"

There was silence. Then reluctantly, Teller snapped, "Salty made up sloppy joes."

"That sounds great. Come along and sit with me."

The boy almost moved to walk along, then said, "No."

Automatically, Bob corrected, "No, thanks."

"No, you bas—"

Without undue effort, Bob snared Teller and took the boy under his arm. With a light knuckle rub, Bob advised, "That kind of language isn't allowed on this place. Watch it." And he released the boy. Then dismissing the discipline, Bob asked, "What'd you have for dessert?"

The kid stood mutinously still.

"I asked." Bob stood there, lax.

Teller was silent.

Bob nudged softly. "And I'm bigger."

"Ice cream."

"Come along and share mine."

There was no reply.

Bob let it go.

But then, later, he whistled and hollered between cupped hands, "Teller!"

And the boy appeared almost right next to Bob. Bob laughed. "You're a genie?"

Teller's face turned hostile. He snarled. "I'm no girl!" He turned away furiously.

Bob caught the boy's arm in a steel grip but his voice was calm. "A genie is a magical male from the *Arabian Nights*. That's a book of stories. We have a copy in the library. I read it when I was your age. Want to come down to the lot with me? I have Mrs. Young's car to see to. It's been missing and coughing."

"Yeah?"

"And she says it goes phooey, snort, phooey, snort!"

Teller almost smiled but he went away.

Bob walked the mile to the lot. It was that kind of town. Teller came along soon afterward. They cleaned points, plugs and carburetor. Then Bob checked the exhaust system and changed some filthy oil.

Bob did the things that needed doing. Teller handed Bob tools and watched and was allowed to go start the engine and to rev it up. They got rid of the phooey, snort. But in the afternoon, Bob had asked, "How's school coming along?"

"Okay."

"You in fifth or sixth grade?"

"Fifth."

"I had a dragon when I was in fifth grade. Her name was Miss Vincent."

Teller exploded, "That's my teacher!" And his eyes were big and horrified.

Bob had had that information from Salty. He smiled at Teller. "Well, do you know what I found out about Miss Vincent?"

Teller's eyes were serious. "What?"

"She's a cream puff if you do your work and listen."

Teller looked at Bob in disgust and didn't comment. But when the car idled smoothly, he was standing slouched, listening, and his thumbs were hung in the edges of his pockets the way Bob's were.

Teller wasn't won. It took patience and tolerance that Bob didn't know how to find. He'd get mad at Teller and yell at him. Then Teller would turn stubborn and obstinate and downright nasty. And he'd vanish.

Salty would ask, "How're you doing with your friend?"

"My *friend?* You're joking." Bob was sour.

"He watches you."

"That's because I had to swat him. He's just being sure I can't get to him by surprise."

"What'd he do?"

"He started the motor when my head was in the engine."

"Uh-oh."

"I was lucky, but he was luckier. After that one pop, he ran. I catch him, I'm going to blister him."

Salty nodded. "I've seldom seen a kid turn so motor crazy all the sudden. Since Georgia's wedding, I've had to buy a lock to keep him out of the tractor. He *really* 'fixed' the mixer for the grain. I just about couldn't figure it out. You ought to teach him basics."

"When I'm calm again, I'll consider it."

Salty didn't even obliquely refer to the fact that Felicia wanted Bob as Papa in the Christmas play. All the rest of September and into October, not once had it been mentioned. Bob was braced and ready to blow up over that very thing, but Salty never said a word. Bob began cautiously to relax. But he still had to watch Teller like a hawk and never put his head under the hood of any of the cars until he knew exactly where Teller was.

Bob had been home for almost three months by then. He was more relaxed and easier without realizing it. He worked hard, earned his keep, paid his bills and banked some money. It felt a little strange to be solvent again.

Two

Then on a perfect Indian summer day toward the end of October, when the trees were gaudy in their fall dress, Bob went down to the car lot to work on Mr. Sanders's old car. He found the hood already up, and a pair of long jeaned legs and the heavy boots of Teller hanging out from the hood-mouth of that old car.

Bob saw that Teller was into another client car, on his own. And he had been expressly forbidden to do that.

Bob took four long strides as he thinned his lips, lifted his hand and really swatted Teller's backside, making him straighten in guilt and crack his head on the underside of the hood.

Bob's hand stung in a very satisfactory way. Hot-eyed with temper, he waited for the boy to withdraw from the car's innards. Teller emerged with some care and had put one slender hand on his backside before he turned to face Bob. And Bob took a deep breath to read the riot act to the kid, when he saw red hair....

Bob blinked. Red hair? Teller's hair was black. Red?

The furious face of the assistant director of the theater group appeared. She said through her teeth, "What is the matter with you? How *dare* you?"

Bob's mouth opened agape and his eyes didn't blink as he stared.

She drew a hand clear down to the back of her knee, and she swung it around, aiming right for him, and it would have landed perfectly, but in some surprise, he pulled back at the last minute. She was so intent on hitting him that she was off balance, and he had to reach out and steady her.

Bob had never seen a woman so mad. It was amazing. He said, "I didn't know it was you."

That did not help anything. "You only hit selected people?"

And Bob got a little defensive. "On occasion, I'll swat a recalcitrant child. What were you doing in that car?"

"I'm a mechanic."

He laughed unkindly.

She said, "Get away from me."

That made him indignant. He replied tartly, "I'm working on this car. This is my father's place. I am his son. I work on the cars."

"Your father has used my ability with cars for several years." Her lips were thinned down and her words were terse. "I was chosen to see to Mr. Sanders's car. Get away from here before I call Salty."

Bob was exasperated—but his palm still stung and he thought about her backside with the red imprint of a hand. His hand. Bob shifted to give himself some time to reorganize his defense, and he saw Teller standing to one side, absolutely fascinated.

It was then that Bob understood why Teller had suddenly become interested in motors. He had a crush on what's-her-name.

Bob put his still-stinging hand on his hip and felt very uncomfortable that he'd popped a woman that way. He shook his head once and cast a quick glance at Teller. With the boy so zombied over the redhead, it was obvious that he'd just arrived. Otherwise, Teller would have come to the redhead's rescue and jumped her "attacker".

Why wasn't Teller in school? Then Bob admonished himself: solve one problem at a time. "What's your name?" Bob finally asked the redhead. Bob swore the question startled her. He was supposed to know her? He squinted his eyes as he racked his brain. Nothing.

"It's none of your business," she snapped.

With her retort, Teller now had a hostile eye bent on Bob.

Bob understood Teller for he had once been twelve and in love with an older woman who had been eighteen. He'd already begun to explain the mistake, "I though you were—" and Bob's hand had started gesturing toward Teller when he realized what it would do to Teller to be called a "kid" in front of her and be identified as one who wasn't allowed inside a car hood unsupervised. So Bob allowed his hand to go on, in an awkward motion, to the top of his head, which he rubbed as he sought words. "I am sorry."

"Where is your keeper?" She was tight-lipped and indignant.

She was just so sassy. He sniped back at her. "Who has you on leash?"

"I take care of myself."

They were standing there, facing each other with their hands on their hips. One of her hands was curled into a fist, the other was flat and back a bit onto the still-stinging mark. They were leaning forward just a bit with their exchange when Salty drove up.

In good weather, nobody ever drove anywhere in Temple unless they were disabled. Anyone driving might miss a greeting and a bit of gossip. But today Salty had uncharacteristically driven over. Bob looked away from the redhead and frowned at his father.

"Well," said his cheery father. "I see you've met your match."

And the redhead demurred. "Only he has struck a blow."

"No!" Salty had witnessed the entire episode from the front porch with Navy binoculars. That's why he was there.

Bob started again, "I thought—" But he couldn't explain while Teller was still standing there, with his fists clenched. Bob said, "I didn't know who was under the hood and I didn't know she had your permission. You might have mentioned you had an unusual mechanic."

"Unusual?" Her voice tested the unpalatable word.

"Female." Bob supplied in a brief aside with barely a glance in her direction.

She almost exploded.

Teller came forward a hesitant step, but Salty stopped him with a glance.

Then Salty went over and kissed the redhead's cheek. "G'morning, darling. Did the brute hurt you?"

"Yes."

In a totally reasonable and kind voice, Salty assured her, "I'll bend him for you."

Teller made a satisfied sound that drew a scowl from Bob, and the redhead said, "Do it."

Bob's very own father *considered* that. Then he said thoughtfully, "I can't bend him in public. The kid's thirty years old, you know."

"How could a son of yours behave in such a nasty way?"

Salty cast an amused glance at Bob and alibied shamelessly, "He's been away from home for twelve years. I've lost control."

"Oh, for Pete's sake!" Bob said with exasperation. Then he told her, "Go home and sit in a tub of ice!" He went to the car but turned back. "Head first."

She asked prissily of Salty, "This person *is* your son?"

Bob's father lifted his eyebrows and both hands in total innocence. "Felicia swore it."

The redhead took several impatient, disbelieving breaths and worked her tightly closed lips before she finally admitted, "Felicia would never lie."

Salty comforted her. "He's a throwback."

"That's the only possible explanation. Let's run him out of town."

Salty sadly shook his head. "I can't. Felicia needs him to play Papa in the Christmas pl—"

"No."

Salty looked at his son in surprise. "You're hesitant?"

And for the first time in his life, Bob realized his mother was only an amateur in acting. Salty had probably been coaching her since their first meeting long ago in a play. Felicia had always made it sound as if Salty had been a muscled stage prop and she the brilliant, budding actress. Bob had just had proof that Felicia couldn't touch her husband's talent.

Bob said in a stern, level, everyday way, "I will not be in that play."

The redhead said in a rush of relieved breath, "Well, thank God for that!"

Bob was a little indignant. "You're not directing. Mother is."

"I'm playing Mama."

"Oh?" His breath froze in his chest and he became a little light-headed. He was alarmed until he realized it was in reaction to the knowledge that he'd made a lucky escape. It was just a good thing he'd already rejected playing Papa, because there was no way in this world that he was going to get into a bed with that redheaded hellcat—even on a stage in front of a packed house. *Particularly* on a stage in front of a packed house!

"Okay." Without even arguing about it, his father gave up and turned from Bob. "Hello, Teller. Taking sides?"

"Yeah."

"Yeah... what?"

"Yes, sir."

"Want to drive yourself back to school?"

"Yeah!"

"Yeah... what?"

"Yes, *sir!*"

Salty turned and smiled benignly at the two antagonists. "See you at lunch."

"He's twelve." Bob felt the need to point that out to his father.

Salty looked at Teller with great surprise. Then he explained, "Well, he can reach the pedals and still see over the steering wheel. Let's go."

Teller started to get in at the driver's side and Salty just waited. Teller glanced over, noticed, then went around the car and opened the door for Salty. Obviously, Teller had driven Salty before then. Bob remembered learning those very rules. Salty got into the passenger side, Teller closed the door carefully, and went back around to get into the driver's seat.

The motor roared into life. Salty said something. Teller adjusted the seat. Then they bucked and inched out of the lot to stop at the road until it was thoroughly scoped out. That done, they jerked and squeaked brakes out onto the road. But before they got too far, Salty turned his head and gave the two witnesses a dancing-eyed speaking glance.

And Bob laughed. He turned to share the humor with the redhead, but she was back under the hood. Bob didn't know what to do. He wanted to rub her backside to comfort the sting he'd laid on her, but he figured she might not accept that kind of sympathy. He knew darned well she wouldn't. She'd blow her red top.

After an awkward pause, Bob asked, "Need any help?"

From under the hood, she replied a very positive "No."

He wandered around looking at the clean new cars on the lot, then entered the showroom where the lone salesman was shining the two cars parked inside. "I didn't know Dad had a woman working the engines."

Rick looked up. "What?"

"The redhead. I didn't know Dad had hired a woman mechanic."

"Yeah."

"Where's she from?"

"Here."

"Here?" His mind scurried over the families and couldn't locate one single redhead. "What's her name?"

"Jo."

"No. I meant her last name."

"Malone."

"Joe? That's a dumb name for her."

"Short for Josephine."

"Oh. Jo."

Rick looked over at Bob in a quizzical way. Then he went on polishing.

"You're going to shine the finish off that car." Bob frowned at his own restlessness.

"Go out and run in some customers."

"It's going to start raining pretty soon. I have to call Mrs. Carstairs and tell her that gas guzzler is going to cost her a new transmission. I can't do anything about it any more. She'll hightail it over here to argue, and with the rain, I'll tell her to come inside, and you've got her."

"I've talked myself blue in the face." Rick shook his head.

"Don't talk. Shine. Stand back and admire. Get in and turn on the radio. Whistle along. You'll drive her crazy."

Rick quit shining and turned to study Bob. "Where'd you learn that?"

"Sales course for computers."

"It'll work with cars?"

Bob shrugged. "It's a variation on technique. I don't see why it wouldn't work."

"Is . . . the transmission really bad?"

"You've known me all my life. I wouldn't pull anything like that."

"We-ll." Rick went over and looked at the sky. "How long would you guess? She'll walk, you know. I can't have her getting wet."

"Want me to go get her?"

Rick looked unsure. "I think she'd be insulted if we offered."

Bob smiled. "Then I'll just tell her it's due to rain pretty soon. That'll hustle her along."

Reflectively, Rick commented, "I went out east to visit some distant relatives, and you know something? The citizens in this town are strange."

That information didn't jar Bob at all. "No. The whole country is. You have to realize all the people who colonized this country were misfits over there on the other side of the ocean. Those in the Midwest are just a bit more eccentric than the easterners because we couldn't stand the people on the east coast and moved out here to get away from them."

"You may be right." Then Rick laughed. "What does that make the people on the west coat?"

"Everybody knows about the people on the west coast. I'll call Mrs. Carstairs."

Bob did that. Mrs. Carstairs agreed to come for a consultation. She'd be about fifteen minutes. Bob smiled at the lowering sky. Then, as a good citizen, Bob went out and approached Jo Malone, the red-headed terror. She came out from under that hood as if she'd expected him to swat her again. That irritated

Bob. He asked, "Want to take the car inside? It's going to rain."

Did she thank him? No. She was primly positive. "No."

That was probably the only word she knew. But she did look at the sky and judge it. Then she ducked back under the hood and ignored him. He could have vanished off the face of the earth, right then, and she would never have turned a hair.

She was just like his ex-wife. Women were a breed unto themselves and it was sad that men were stuck with them. That is to say, that *other* men were stuck with them. Bob Brown didn't want to deal with any female. He was through with women.

He walked across the lot to Mrs. Carstairs's car and scowled at it. Good car. It had served its time. It had three hundred eighty-three thousand miles on it. That ought to be enough for any car. Absentmindedly, he patted the hood before he got into the car and drove it into the garage and up on the rack. He got out and operated the hoist, lifting the car up so that its underside was exposed.

He walked over to the doorway and leaned his shoulder against the opening frame and noted the approaching storm. Then he watched for Mrs. Carstairs to approach. When he finally saw her striding along, he strolled out to meet her at the edge of the lot.

"Well, Bob."

That was her greeting. He smiled back. "Did you bring an umbrella?"

"No. I'm going to drive home."

"Not without a new transmission."

"I'll do that, then."

"I've put the car up on the rack to show you what all these years have done to the bottom of your car. The road salt in the winters has been your enemy."

He showed her. He was so concentrated in communicating the fragility of the car and the futility of using any more money on it, that he didn't notice when Jo came along and stood silently observing, listening.

Bob had to raise his voice to be heard over the rumbling of thunder. The lights dimmed as they sometimes did with storms. Mrs. Carstairs never said a word.

"If you drove this car out of town, I would worry about you. You need to promise me that you won't leave Temple, driving this car. Your solemn promise."

She sighed hugely. "Well, I guess that you'd best show me that red car you have inside."

Bob was stunned. His mouth opened and he couldn't think of a thing to say. Finally he came up with, "You're smarter than I thought."

Mrs. Carstairs laughed and shared her delight with Jo, who was watching Bob.

Bob escorted Mrs. Carstairs over to the inside door that led from the garage into the showroom. "You remember Rick?"

"Yes. How're the kids?"

"Fine." Rick smiled as he interrupted his whistling and continued to shine the gray car, stepping back to admire it and wipe a shiny spot that didn't need it.

"Rick. Mrs. Carstairs would like to see the red car."

Rick gave Bob a blank look, and Bob could see Rick's gears change as he began to smile, just a little, then he beamed and said, "A great little car. Come see it."

Bob closed the door and went back to the white elephant still up on the rack. He lowered it to ground level and stood looking at it seriously and a little sadly as he gave the hood another sympathetic pat.

Jo said, "A good car."

Bob was so lost in his thoughts that he only nodded and added, "In its day. It's the road salt that . . ." He turned his head and stared. She'd spoken to him voluntarily?

But she was disappearing down the hall to the supply room. The lights went out. That was not unusual in Temple.

Bob caught up a flashlight and went down the hall. "Jo?" It was the first time he'd said her name to her. It seemed meaningful to do that. Different from any other time he'd said a woman's name to the woman. How strange. He called again, "Jo?"

A little voice said, "I'm here."

There was an earth-ending crash of thunder that would make a believer out of just about anyone. Bob said, "Me and You, Lord." And he laughed to share the shiver such a storm gave anybody.

She was about as big-eyed as she could be and she was holding onto a shelf and trembling. She was scared? Jo Malone the Terror? Making his voice very calm and comforting, Bob said, "It's sure noisy, isn't it?"

With the ground reacting to the power of the storm, the metal things on the shelves clinked and rattled. She shivered. Bob said, "Come into the hall. You won't be as vulnerable there as you are here with all this metal clanking and dancing around."

He gently took her arm and, walking backward, facing her, he tugged her after him back into the hall. "My sister, Georgia, used to get under the bed."

Jo didn't reply. Her hand was like ice. How could she be so afraid? Little Miss Terror? That was such a surprise. She had seemed invincible. He sat the flashlight on the floor so that it wasn't pitch dark before he said, "I was in a tornado once."

Her convulsive shudder in response to that opening gambit stopped it cold. He tried again to distract her. "Have you lived here in Temple all along?"

She nodded in little shakes.

"How could I have missed you?"

"You're older."

He heard her teeth rattle as she looked out toward the garage. "Do you want to go into the showroom? Rick and Mrs. Carstairs are in there."

"Glass."

He thought she wanted a drink of water and started to move to the fountain. That's when he discovered she was holding onto his shirt sleeve. She was so discreet about it that he hadn't known until then. Somehow that pleased him. Then his compassion was caught and he said, "This is the safest place you could be."

She didn't respond, so he said, "I'm here. You're safe and sound."

She looked at him in complete disbelief.

He could get some reaction from her. She wasn't completely terrified, so he chatted to distract her. "You said I'm older. I'm not that old. Why don't I remember you?"

"You've been gone."

"I've been back since August. How old are you?"

She was young enough she didn't mind such an obtuse question. "Twenty-three."

He smiled. "Young."

That gave her a distracting irritation.

"You go to mechanics school?"

"My dad had a filling station."

"Oh, yeah. I remember that. Over on the east side. You still have it?"

"He died. Mother wasn't interested in keeping it, and I was away at school."

"Why'd you come back?"

She shrugged. "I know all the people—"

An ear-splitting crash interrupted.

She made such a brief, tiny, pitiful smothered sound. And he felt as if he could hold up all the walls all by himself. "Hey, Jo. It's really okay." And he started to put his arms around her.

She straight-armed him and said, "No!"

That surprised him. And it made him a little indignant. He was just trying to comfort her. "Okay!" He turned away from her and put his hands into his pockets. He walked to the end of the hall and watched as the water poured from the sky and the lightning flashed worldwide.

After a time, he said neutrally, "This'll fill the gully."

There was no reply. He turned back. "Jo?"

In the glow of the flashlight, she was crouched down by the wall with her arms over her head.

Bob went over and squatted down beside her. He took her into his arms and held her on his lap between him and the wall. He sang "Rain, rain, go away—" and her breathing changed. She was crying?

She was rigid. He very carefully insinuated his head between her head clamped to her shoulder and said, "This is a waste of time. You need some therapy if you're like this for just a little storm. Do you realize this will probably turn to sleet at this time of the year? Then it'll snow, and we'll have one hell of a mess. Everyone will finally be coming in for their antifreeze and driving us crazy wanting their snow tires on. Do you know that? How are you at putting on snow tires? I'll bet your car is the first one here tomorrow and you'll be mad because we can't get to it for all the damned phone calls."

And for a man who was through with women, this one on his lap became very vividly female. And he had no urgent impulse to get her off his lap and get away from her. She was all woman. That was obvious.

Women just feel different. She was curled up, but the side of her breast was against the side of his chest and his chest got excited and communicated that fact to the rest of his body. She smelled different. She didn't smell at all like any man he'd ever known. She smelled only faintly of femaleness so that his nose was trying to breathe in more of her.

He was shocked that he wanted to nudge around with his face against her and just inhale the scent of her. He felt shivers up his back and he licked his lips quickly and swallowed.

He had to control his lap and he had to shift her a little. His hands loved the job of shifting her and he had to make them behave because they wanted to do some other shifting. So he coughed a little and cleared his throat and talked.

He knew when she began to relax. He went right on talking. He told all the preparations for winter that hadn't been done. "You'd think we didn't know winter was coming," he told her. "Abner still hasn't painted the house and the storm windows haven't been put in yet." He talked about such mundane things that the next really serious thunder only made her jerk a little. But her breathing was still a little fast.

When the storm finally moved on north and east, out past Cleveland and over Lake Erie, he asked, "What in the world happened that made you that scared of storms?"

But she only released herself from him. She was apparently so embarrassed that even in just the flashlight, he could see that she blushed.

So he distracted her a bit more. "Are you a real redhead?"

That did stir her. "Good grief."

"Do you shave—"

"No!"

"—your armpits?"

She clamped her lips together and seemed to be really irritated with him.

He smiled.

"There is no need for you to laugh at me!"

His voice became very gentle. "I wasn't. I meant only to distract you. I know what it's like to be scared. I got help with mine."

It took a while, but she finally looked up. "I can't believe you'd be afraid of anything."

"We all have our Achilles' heels."

"Most people can control their fear."

He nodded. "You need to talk to someone. Maybe a weatherman."

She gave him a really very patient look. But her regard became different. And her own voice was serious when she said, "Thank you."

"Who generally holds your hand?"

"I do."

"An iron woman?" he guessed.

"There's no one else."

"Your mother?"

Jo shook her head. "She went to live with my brother."

"That was John?"

"Yes."

"I remember him."

"His wife ran off with another man and left him with the kids."

"I'm glad your mother went and not you."

"Why do you say that?" she asked.

"It's a rough life for a young woman to be harnessed with another woman's responsibilities that way."

"Look at your family. Look at all the 'other women's' kids your parents have raised."

"They do it together. That's different."

"I used to long to belong to Felicia and Salty. There was always shouting and laughter."

"We have some dandy fights. You should see Salty then! He's really tough. And there's Teller. He has a crush on you. Did you know? That's why I couldn't say that I thought he was the one under the car hood. Not in front of him. And I'm sorry I swatted you. He'd been forbidden to get into cars on his own. He doesn't know enough about them. He's zonked on you. I think it's that red hair of yours."

"My curse." She sighed forlornly.

"Curse? Why's that?"

"In our family, the redheads always end up bad."
She looked at her fingers. Her voice accepted that
premise was so.

He scoffed. "Obligated to go wrong?"

"I don't know."

"I'd be happy to oblige in any way I can to bring
about your downfall." He grinned.

She said very sadly, "It isn't funny."

"Honey, I don't believe I've ever seen a more
straightlaced woman in all my life. There is no dan-
ger, at all, of you going—what was it—bad? That's
just silly."

"How glib you are."

"If I'd been glib I wouldn't have had all the trou-
bles that I've had." He looked aside grimly.

"You wouldn't recognize trouble if it sat on your
lap."

He did hear her. And he considered that she had
been on his lap very recently. The statement did give
him pause. Was she "trouble"? Hardly. Even if he
wanted trouble from her, she wouldn't be willing to
cooperate. No one gets into trouble all by himself. Or
even herself.

She thought being a redhead was a curse. If he could
recall correctly, back in history, the English once
thought red hair was a curse. It was amazing the things
that spooked people. Mostly silly things. Redheads
cursed? Now, that was nonsense.

He looked at her smooth red hair that was strag-
gling from the knot on the top of her head. He'd like
to put his hands into that mass and kiss her until her
eyes . . . What on earth was he thinking?

Here she thought she was "cursed" with red hair.
He was cursed with body hunger. And looking at her,
he could feel the delicious ache he'd been ignoring.

Men had it tough.

Three

———

Waiting for the rain to quit, Mrs. Carstairs had to have all the information about her new car, and she told stories about her faithful old car.

Bob had to discourage her from having the old car smashed into a cube and using it as a coffee table. "The weight," he explained. "The floor would need to be shored up, and you have the recreation room just below your living room. You can't have beams put in the middle of the floor that way. It'd ruin your shuffleboard game." Mrs. Carstairs gave up the idea with great reluctance.

So it was a little late that noon when Bob walked home in the brisk wind that had followed the impressive cloudburst that morning. The wind had shifted to the northwest. Summer had had one of her last encores. Winter was coming.

Since the Brown house was just outside the south edge of the little town, Bob had to leave the gravel road for a short lane, and he had time to study the pile of boards that was home to the Browns and their accumulated family.

The house and ten acres were really a strange mix of eccentricity and trash. Luty, who did their carpentry repairs, had kept up with most of the problems. Not the barn. He wouldn't touch the barn. It tilted. Several times a year the family would have a rather static debate on whether the barn was at a stable period or if it had tilted just a bit more.

Bob eyed the house and accepted the fact that he was as responsible as anyone for not getting the storm windows up. He'd get that organized this afternoon. As he walked up to the house, he began counting the appalling number of windows.

Salty was the only one left in the kitchen. He was preparing a hunk of pork to slowly roast for supper. As his father rubbed the seasonings into the meat, Bob inquired, ''Does my mother know that you go around kissing redheads?''

In his rasping voice, and with a really very subtle version of a wide theatrical gesture, Bob's father replied, ''It's the theater influence. You have to know that.'' Then his eyes glinted just one diamond light as he asked in turn, ''Does my knowing little Jo Malone and being allowed to kiss her cheek rankle in you?''

Shortly, Bob replied, ''No.''

''She is a jewel-child,'' Salty touched the gentle words with his raspy voice softened.

''She thinks the red hair is a curse.''

''No!''

Bob watched as, with that single word, Salty had paused and lifted his head like a carefully tempered iron man who was therefore a trustworthy leader. How'd he do that? Was he really such a man? Or was Bob still seeing his father as the hero he'd always expected? Was it all a facade?

Salty asked, "Who told Jo that red hair was a curse?"

"I don't know. But they convinced her that she'll go bad."

"Blast the bitch or bastard who did that to such a sweet child."

"Agreed."

Salty dished up the homemade vegetable soup in companionable silence. He served it to Bob with crusty rolls. Then as Bob ate with savoring, Salty put the huge roast into the oven and set the heat very low. By suppertime, the aroma would have driven them all to salivating and pacing like restless dogs.

Salty offered, "Teller did go back to school this morning."

"How'd you do that?"

"I let him drive me there."

"It's against the law for a kid that age to drive." Bob knew that his father was well aware of that fact.

"I asked Pete to allow it because it's the only way I can get to the boy." Pete was Temple's Chief of Police.

"Where'd you get him?"

"Remember Lanny? He was here just before you were ten."

"Yeah. Great guy."

Salty agreed. "He is. He's involved with juvenile delinquents now in Cleveland and he especially asked us to take Teller."

"Any particular problem?"

Salty put his hands on his hips and his raspy voice growled. "Abused in a lot of different ways. We have to help him adjust to going back and being a child a little longer. He's been on the streets."

"How's his influence with the other kids?" Bob looked up at his dad.

Salty sighed in a long gust and shook his head in two or three slow turns of concern. "That's always a worry, but Teller isolates himself. He's reluctant to enter into the general activities the kids cook up. He feels like an outsider. We have to help him join in."

Bob walked right into it. "How're you going to do that?"

His father didn't even hesitate. "He's going to be in the Christmas play... with you."

Bob had started nodding, agreeing that Teller should be in the play; but the stinger stopped that and Bob stared at his father, digruntled. "You did it to me."

Salty agreed. "I needed the right buttons. You're a pushover for a human in trouble."

A little nastily, Bob asked, "Is that why Jo was under that car hood this morning? You wanted to drag her across my trail and solve us both?"

His father looked so genuinely shocked, so subtly astounded over such an idea, that Bob narrowed his eyes and searched for a clue. Was his dad that good an actor? My God, what a waste if he was.

Salty was saying, "You're the only one the kid watches. If you agree to play Papa, we might get him to be the lead reindeer, prancing and pawing. He'll get to wear antlers.''

But Bob interrupted with gritty insolence. ''If I agree to be Papa, then Papa gets to kiss Mama goodnight when he gets into bed.''

The only betrayal was the appreciative gleam that briefly lit his father's eyes. Salty's face didn't change one bit. He considered the request. ''Maybe.'' He drew the contemplation out for the perfect amount of time before he said, ''It would be good theater.''

''Be sure it's in the script and directions. If it isn't, I walk.'' Bob's face was stony.

''In Boston, were you on the bargaining board?'' his father asked with courteous interest.

''No,'' Bob replied shortly.

''You handled this very well.''

Bob cast a suspicious glance at his tricky father.

Salty observed with thoughtful consideration, ''I don't see any objection to such a change.''

''Don't tell Jo ahead of time.''

''Ahh.''

''What's that mean?''

''That stupid man out east whose daughter rejected you, how's his business going?''

The company loyalty still clung to Bob. ''Not well.''

''You made a lucky escape.''

Those rasping words were very soothing. Would the day ever come when he could talk about that terrible time to his dad? Not discussing it, but spilling all that poisonous sludge from his soul to his listening father. To tell him of the bitterness? The shock of it all. Going from being an integral part of something to figuratively being left alone on a bare and vacant plain. All he'd built had disintegrated right before his eyes, and he had been as helpless to prevent any of it as he would in trying to shape water with his hands. How could he have been so blind? So stupid?

"Bob... You've been off somewhere."

"Yeah."

"Do you wanta talk yet?" The rasp was gentled.

Bob shook his head once and didn't look up. "No."

His father allowed a brief silence in case the refusal would be breached. It was not, so he said, "I washed the storm windows this morning. The kids should help put them up after school."

"Okay."

Salty was at the window and saw Jo coming up the lane. He said to Bob, "Nobody brought in the eggs this morning. They were all late and disorganized, and I forgot to remind them. Would you do that?"

Bob sighed, wiped his mouth and folded his napkin into the holder before he got up and put his dishes into the dishwasher. "Yeah." Thirty years old and he still had to go out and hunt the damned eggs. Why couldn't the hens be penned? Felicia couldn't *stand* for anything to be confined. So the hens laid their eggs in hidden nests. It was a big irritation. Bob looked at his father and was suddenly aware he was no longer a young man. His voice a little gruff, Bob said, "The soup was special. I forget what a good cook you are."

"You don't need to leave a tip."

Bob touched the older man's shoulder. "I'll go get the eggs."

"Use the front door. I saw one of the hens out by the tractor and heard it clucking this morning."

Bob obediently headed that way and was already on the porch when his glance was drawn to the approaching figure. Jo. He looked back at the house.

Had his father seen her? How was he to know? Well. If there was an egg under the tractor, the old man would be innocent.

Jo's footsteps hesitated as she saw Bob. He stood and waited. In the crisper air, she wore a thigh-length coat and her head was wrapped in a scarf. Her cheeks were pink and she wore big glasses. She looked like a winterized bug.

He said, "Hello, Jo." Yeah. Brilliant. He was disgusted with himself.

There was a tiny empty silence. Her words were a challenge. "Why aren't you downtown at Joe's Bar and Grill with all the other men?"

"I had to come home and hunt up the eggs."

She snorted in disbelief.

"You don't believe me."

She shook her head.

"Then come along and watch." He never took his hard look from her face. After her taunting question, she was almost committed to letting him prove that silly statement about hunting the eggs. If she did, he had her.

"Still no hen houses?"

"You know that Felicia believes in freedom. The hens make their own nests wherever they want."

She tilted her head back in an acknowledging single nod.

Bob went to the tractor, and Jo trailed along after him with marked hesitation. He carefully examined the drying grasses protected by the tractor's bulk. He saw the deliberate grass arrangement by one tire, went around the tractor and ducked under it at that wheel. Inside the careful nest, there was an egg.

Mentally, Bob apologized to his father for thinking the old man was a conniving plotter. He showed the egg to Jo. "Brown." He made the unnecessary comment. "Any Brown is the best." He meant that he was.

She took the literal meaning. "There's no difference except in the color of the shell."

He dismissed such a comment. "You've never made a real testing or you wouldn't say that."

So she moved a little snippily as they went to the barn. It was the next logical place to look at that time of year. And inside, Bob was congratulating himself on how astutely he was handling this prickly woman. He'd get a kiss, just watch. He looked around the interior and said, "Well, where do you think is the best place to look?"

"In the corners?"

He nodded as he considered that. Did he dare lure her up into the loft? Naw. Better wait. "I'll pay a forfeit for every egg you find."

"What." There was no questioning. Her single word was for clarification. She wanted to know the forfeit.

He smiled. "I'll think of something."

Again, even more cautiously, she said, "What."

He gestured and grinned. "You could work toward a free lube job?" He looked quickly to see her reaction. She was a mechanic.

But she took him literally and thought about it. She moved a little as if she might leave, right then, but she didn't. That amazed Bob. He was astonished she had even come to the barn with him. Was he *that* safe looking? Hell.

Not only Helen, the cow, but the pony and nanny goat had to come into the barn to see what the people were doing. So they had to be petted and talked to before they'd leave the people alone.

The pair found more nests, and Bob had to get a basket to hold the eggs. Jo busily put straw into the basket in order to cushion them.

Altogether, they found almost a dozen. One was a little heavy and so it was questionable. Probably rotten. He said she could carry that one.

"Never mind."

"We have to keep it separate," he explained. "Think how the kitchen would smell if Salty opened it for breakfast!"

"I'll carry the basket—you take the egg."

"I've never seen such big glasses. You look like a bug."

"How flattering."

Bob laughed. "There are sayings like 'cute as a bug.'"

"I have never found bugs appealing."

He smiled down at her and told her softly, "You should be standing here, looking at you."

"Now, that was smooth."

"Take off your glasses. You're looking a little cross-eyed."

"You're too close."

"Oh, no."

"Back off." She frowned at him.

"I can't."

"You have me against the wall. Back off."

Bob looked up in elaborate surprise. "Now, how did that happen?" But he didn't move back. "Let me have a very little kiss, and I'll carry the rotten egg."

"Back off or you'll be *wearing* the rotten egg."

He grinned. "Sassy." However reluctantly, he moved back and freed her.

"Do we have them all?" She lifted the basket to indicate the eggs.

"We didn't check the loft." He smiled like a satyr, a goat man.

She gave him a drolly patient look. "I'll wait here."

So he had to go up and hunt around. He did that with dispatch. And he did find another nest. "Would you believe it? One of those hens came up here!"

"Just one?"

"Umm." He looked farther. But in that quick scan, he didn't see another. "I don't think they always remember where they hide them." He climbed down the ladder and put the egg with the rest in her basket.

She smiled at the largess. "This has been nice. I haven't hunted eggs since the Easter I was eight."

Expansively generous, he said, "Anytime you get the urge, come on out."

"Thank you."

"You really are welcome. Did you come out to see Salty or Felicia?"

"Why do you call them by their first names?"

"Most people do." He shrugged. "The kids who live here do. It becomes almost automatic. In serious times, it's Dad and Mother."

"They are unusual people. You are fortunate."

"We do realize that. On occasion, they can be very irritating. They can also be a little too theatrical."

"They're brilliant." She became earnest. "I would love to direct them in some of the Alfred Lunt and Lynn Fontanne plays. Even Salty's injured voice would be perfect. They are extraordinarily masculine and feminine. And they are so skilled."

"So. You recognize that Salty's an actor?" How could she already know that when he'd just discovered it?

She moved and opened out her hand in a modest sweep. "Who could not?"

He hadn't. He brushed that fact aside and said, "I've consented to be Papa in the play."

She looked at him, bug-eyed again, but she didn't say anything.

He said, "We need to practice."

"What? We have no dialogue. All I do is lie in bed. You do the running around. All you have to do is listen to the narrator."

"I need to practice... getting *into* bed."

She was twenty-three. She recognized a lecher. Her eyelashes closed down and her mouth looked skeptical as she put her head side to side in a "yeah, sure" manner. But she did smile just a bit.

She pushed past him and went out of the barn, carrying the egg basket. Less eagerly, Bob followed, carrying the rotten egg.

At the house, Salty exclaimed over the egg largess, and confirmed the one was rotten. There was another iffy one and both were carefully buried.

Felicia drifted downstairs and the four sat down to talk. The Christmas play was mentioned, and Bob said, "Mother, I'll be Papa."

She put a hand to her throat and looked stricken. "Oh, my dear boy, why *couldn't* you have agreed sooner?"

"What do you mean?" Bob's question was cautious.

Her voice trembling with emotion, Felicia told the terrible news. "I convinced Porter that he could do it."

"Porter?"

Hitting the bottom notes of her marvelous range, Felicia confirmed her word. "Porter."

Bob protested. "With Porter on the stage for a Christmas play, the audience will be so amazed that they won't take their eyes off him, and they'll all whisper, 'There's Porter!' and 'Is that *Porter* up there?' and 'I can't believe Porter would be in a *Christmas* play.' and 'How could that possibly be Porter?' Then the whispering will overwhelm the narrator and none of the participants will know what they're supposed to be doing. You will wreak havoc. You can't have Porter."

Jo considered that, for drama, Felicia and Salty's eldest son was no slouch.

"But, darling," Felicia protested modestly but in despair. "I convinced him that he wants to do it! How can I possibly take this away from him?"

Bob soothed his mother. "I'll handle it."

His mother said uncertainly, "I don't recall you being particularly tactful. Have you acquired that talent? Porter is very sensitive."

Bob snorted.

Jo said thoughtfully, "Porter's so big that he'll make the bed sag, and I'll roll right over on top of him."

Bob stared at her, "seeing" her on top of Porter. More firmly, Bob said, "Porter hasn't the talent to be Papa. I'll convince him of it."

Bob did notice, in a small part of his mind, that not once did his father and mother exchange so much as a glance.

Jo said, "You're sure you can convince him? Do you mind being Papa?"

Bob sighed in resignation. "If Porter should do the part, the play will be ruined. Being in the play is important to a lot of the kids." He gave a stern glance at Salty to make his father remember that Teller was supposed to participate.

Salty's raspy comment was a perfect balance between acknowledging a "forgotten" reminder and dedication to the cause. "Thanks, son, do your best to convince Porter. I'm surprised at you, Felicia, you didn't tell me you were asking Porter."

Her gesture was restrained agitation. "I was simply *desperate* and I saw him downtown, stooped over, squinting into the hardware store window. It looked enough like Papa peering out the window—after he throws up the sash, you know. And Porter was nice enough about doing it!" The wonderful voice faltered. "It does seem a shame to discourage him, now."

Bob said firmly, "I'll give his car a free lube job."

But Felicia pushed it. "It was the town's recognition that really bought him. I told Porter that the town would be grateful."

"We'll give him a plaque." Bob decided that.

Salty rasped, "Why?"

That stumped them all.

Before rehearsals began, Bob managed to see Jo twice by "purest accident." The first time, she'd cleaned her little house and had just finished scrubbing her kitchen floor. She was hot and sweaty, her red hair was tumbled and errant curls had slithered down over her forehead and in front of one ear. Bob's eyes got hot and he smiled. "Been busy?"

She stared at him. "How could you be so rude that you'd recognize me this way?"

"This is your house. You answered the door."

"I could be the hired help!"

He slid his hands into his corduroy trouser pockets. He licked his smile and amended his words. "Well, hello, stranger. New in town?"

"Next door, Mrs. Thomas is upstairs with her chin on the windowsill, watching."

"A scandal brewing? What *have* you been doing to look so tumbled about?"

Jo took a deep, very patient breath, which drew Bob's attention to her chest and the sight darted his gaze around blindly. He shifted his feet as she replied, "Every man in town has been clamoring for my attention and I've had to struggle to keep them all at arm's length."

"I believe it."

She frowned a little and asked, "Which do you believe, the clamor or the struggle?"

"Both."

"That might be a compliment, but you have to know that I've been cleaning the house. In just one month, everyone will be coming home for Thanksgiving, and Mother is snide in looking around, checking."

"I could help you."

"How nice of you to offer, now that it's mostly done."

He bit his lip, but his eyes smiled and danced with lights of laughter.

She waited, watching that, then she looked off. "By now, Mrs. Thomas is on the phone to Mrs. Walton. Why are you here?"

"To give you a copy of the script and to do some preliminary rehearsals."

"Oh, yes." She became cautious, watching him warily.

He pulled the "script" from his back pocket and flipped the pages. "Here." He crowded her backward through her doorway, into the kitchen and closed the door behind them.

"When the curtain opens," she said patiently. "I am in bed. And I stay in bed, asleep, during the entire production."

"How much are we paying you for this cushy performance?"

"No one gets any money for this rendition of 'The Night before Christmas.' It's the group's Christmas gift to the town. After the play, we lead the audience in the carols. Just about the entire town is involved."

"Well," Rather ponderously, he paced a step or two. "As Papa, I have to check out the house and then get into bed with my 'wife' and we should practice that." He gave her a bland, attentive, reasonable look of professional diligence. He added, "The play's the thing."

"Clever." She folded her arms over her nice chest.

"All really dedicated actors seize any opportunity to hone their skill."

"At least you didn't say 'practicing their craft.'"

"I grew up with Felicia, if you recall that, and I find that I must have learned a thing or two from her husband—who is my father. I have his genes, also."

"Formidable." She watched him.

He pushed up his lower lip to hide the wolf's smile, but his eyes were filled with laughter. He rubbed his hands together briskly and said, "It's getting really cold. Do you have any coffee left? We could have a cup before we...practice."

"Everything is clean. Even the coffeepot."

With her words, his gaze ran over her tousled hair and down her sweaty body with her T-shirt sticking to her so revealingly. He indicated that she wasn't clean. "Would you like a shower, first?"

"I don't believe we need to practice."

"Ah!" he exclaimed and put a palm on his forehead. "And you a...director?"

"Yes. It *is* my professional opinion that I will be able to be in the bed when the curtain opens and there will be no problem."

"What if I pull the covers off you? What if I swat you on your bottom and say, 'It's Christmas, wife! How about a little?'"

She blushed scarlet.

He laughed wickedly. "I need to know exactly how I should do this."

"What." Only the word. No question. She gave him a cool look.

His attention entirely on Jo, and not on his words, he said, "My wife slept in a separate room. The only time I got into her bed with her was when she was willing. How does a loving man who sleeps with his wife—all the time—get into bed? These are the nuances of portrayal that are important to communicate the atmosphere of the family." He bit his lip again and then said quite seriously, "Does he ignore the fact that he'd probably made the bed shift? That the covers might be pulled from her? Are they good friends?"

With the revelations of his words, her eyes had become serious and her mouth softened. She looked down and turned her head for a minute. "I have an appointment at school in less than an hour. When we begin rehearsals, we'll talk about what you've said. You've made an excellent point."

That surprised him. He'd been taunting her to see what she would do, how she would respond. But then he considered the truth of his words, for her; and he, too, sobered. That his marriage had been bitter and unfriendly was now quite obvious. He blushed a little for revealing so much to her. He, too, turned aside. "I'll see you at rehearsal, then." He looked back at her. Then he smiled just a little. "You're a terror, do you know that? You scare the hell out of me."

And he left.

He walked off her back porch, looked up at Mrs. Thomas's upstairs window and waved, then he shoved his hands into his trouser pockets, hunched his shoulders in his heavy sweater and went back to his car. He got in and drove along, thinking about peeling those damp clothes off Jo's sweaty body and making her even hotter.

Four

But as Bob drove along, the thought crept into his consciousness. He'd betrayed the fact to Jo that his wife hadn't allowed him to sleep in her bed. Such a thing was something a man didn't like known. And, bitterly, Bob dwelled on the disaster of his marriage.

Then niggling in his mind was the thought that he'd seen something. He frowned into the rearview mirror and slowed. Then he turned around and looked back. It had been a figure that had ducked out of sight.

Bob turned the car back, went down the street, looking, then turned the corner and searched. He finally found Teller and trapped him in an alley. He crept the car toward the boy as he ran ahead.

Finally, Bob stopped the car and yelled, "Come back! Salty's on the other street heading this way. If you get in my car and duck down, Salty might not see you."

Teller hesitated, looked for an escape, gave up and lagged his steps coming toward Bob.

Bob reached across and opened the passenger door.

Teller hesitated then came to the driver's side. "I'll drive." It was a try.

Bob's look was enduring. "Get in."

Teller went around the car as if they were old friends who'd planned to meet this way. He got into the car and settled. "How come you're driving? Nobody drives in this town in good weather."

"I was looking for you," Bob lied. "Why aren't you in school?"

Teller sighed enormously. "They do dumb things there that take too much time. I don't need that stuff."

"What stuff." Bob didn't question, he simply nudged with the words.

"I don't know any reason for me to go to school. I heard this country was started so people can do what they want. I don't want to go to school."

"At least they've taught you something."

There was a little silence as they drove along. Then Teller's curiosity got the better of him. "What did they teach me?"

"That this is a free country."

"Yeah. And I don't have to—"

"Yes, you do. You're free—right after you finish high school."

"That's..." Teller ran a thumb over his fingers and protested, "seven more years!"

"You can at least figure that out. So you know a little math. What else do you know?"

"Make me go to school, and I'm out of here."

"How's reading?"

"Silly."

"Ever been tested?"

Silently, Teller slumped in the seat and put an ankle on the opposite knee.

"Let's go over to the school and find out how you're doing."

"Don't do that to me."

Bob was very serious. "Did you ever hear what Salty did to me when I was your age and played hooky?"

Curiosity finally made Teller reply, "No."

Bob gave Teller a side look and said, "You don't want to know."

"Tell me."

"You wouldn't be able to eat your lunch."

"You serious?"

And Bob's face was bland. "Would I lie?"

"Everybody lies."

"What a cynic."

"What's a . . . cynic?"

"Look it up."

At the school, Bob grabbed Teller, who was halfway out of the car before it stopped. Then Bob had to crawl out that side, too, and keep hold of Teller. It was very similar to what Salty had had to do to get Teller into church. They walked up to the school door, and that's when Teller gave up. He said, "Let go."

"Promise you'll stay with me."

Teller looked up. "Yeah. You'll leave me here."

"I promise I'll take you home with me."

"And tell Salty about me being outside." Teller sulked.

"No."

"Then let's just go back now."

"I need some information."

"I haven't been here all week. Now you know. That's what you want, isn't it?"

"Actually, it isn't. Come with me. I want you to sit and behave. Do you understand? I'm threatening you. If you don't behave and sit still, you may find out that I learned terrible things from Salty doing them to me."

"Yeah, you go around popping women on their butts."

"You do know I thought it was you under that hood."

"You ever pop her again and I'll loosen your teeth."

"You're safe with your threat. I felt terrible."

"Well, start worrying about popping me again. I won't let you."

"All you have to do is what you're supposed to do. You behave and you don't get popped. Understand? When you turned on that motor, you could have killed me. If that had happened," he exaggerated the term deliberately, "you'd have gone to prison for life. If you think school's bad, prison is poison."

Teller looked off to the side and didn't reply.

In the school office, Bob found that Teller had been shifted around so much that he hadn't had the opportunity to learn basics at all well. They'd only that week been able to gather his records and figure him out. "We have someone here in Temple who tutors, and she has agreed to see what can be done."

"And I'm dumb." Teller shouted that, standing up with his fists clenched and his face furious.

Mrs. Staffer said calmly, "No," and she straightened the papers casually.

Bob's hand shot out and took hold of Teller's arm. He said in a perfectly normal voice, "Sit down. You promised. And, Teller, no one has said anything about you being dumb.''

"The kids did.''

"That's because you haven't given them the time to know you. You can learn, just the same way you can learn engines. It takes a little time.''

With Bob's iron grip keeping him from running, Teller subsided back onto the chair, but he was close to furious tears and fighting for control.

Mrs. Staffer said, "That is true. And, Teller, you've been moved around quite a bit, so no one has had the time to help you. We do have all the records, see? All these people were trying to help you. You just weren't there long enough for anyone to get your attention. Miss Malone wants to help.''

Bob was very conscious that Teller took a quick breath at the sound of Jo's name.

Mrs. Staffer was continuing. "She was contacted yesterday and saw the records. She said that your problem isn't serious.''

Teller's voice was a little strident. "What do you mean?''

"It will involve teaching you the basics in phonetics and arithmetic. Miss Malone will help you. You need to be patient. This is more readily done, if you want to do it.''

Bob's mind was still thinking about Teller being with Jo to study. The kid already had a crush on her. This might not be a good idea. "Is there anyone else who could teach him?''

"Salty.''

"Does he know about this?'' Bob gestured to the reports on Mrs. Staffer's desk.

"Of course. It was he who asked for the records to be forwarded here. He knew someone who could expedite that, so we have them very quickly. And, as I said, Salty and Miss Malone saw them yesterday."

"Miss Malone?" Teller's voice was very young.

"Jo Malone," Mrs. Staffer confirmed.

"She . . . knows." Teller said the two words in defeat.

"It's no disgrace." Mrs. Staffer folded her hands and leaned forward kindly. "Everyone has some kind of problem. Mine was math. I still think fractions are stupid." She smiled. "But I learned them. It was a real struggle. It's still a struggle when I use fractions in baking something either more or less than that listed in a recipe."

Teller looked up at Bob in quick curiosity.

Bob looked back. Then he said, "When you can read and do arithmetic to suit Salty, I'll tell you my problem."

Teller's face changed slowly to speculation. Then, when Mrs. Staffer asked him, "Would you like to begin today? Miss Malone is coming here in about twenty-five minutes."

Never taking his eyes off Bob, Teller replied, "Okay."

That entire afternoon, Bob spent pressured time in town and on the phone telling people they must not allow Teller to know about his own learning problem. He neglected to tell Jo Malone.

So Teller came home that afternoon and found Bob hanging up the phone from one more call. Bob eyed a smug-looking Teller and asked, "Are you okay?" The kid looked a little odd.

And Teller lisped "Yeth."

Bob's eyes narrowed. "Who told." It wasn't a question, it was a demand.

"Mith Malone. The thaid you had a thinky time thaying wordth."

"It wasn't fun." Bob was serious. "I'm not allowing you to mock me. I no longer lisp. But while I did, it was an invitation to be taunted."

Teller didn't reply.

"I had to relearn how my tongue was used. I did it."

Teller looked off to the side, then back at Bob. He turned and walked off.

Bob went over to Jo's, walking in the cold, getting control of his temper. He pounded on her kitchen door, and she opened it. She greeted him with, "Mrs. Thomas told me to stay away from you—that you are dangerous."

"Especially now."

"Oh?"

"You told Teller that I lisped."

"I did," she agreed. "He admires you. Before today, only Salty could have gotten Teller back to school. But you did it. Mrs. Staffer called me as soon as you left, so I was a little early. Teller asked me what your problem had been. Mrs. Staffer heard. She told me, 'Bob said when Teller wins the right, Bob will tell him what his own problem was.'"

"So you got Teller off the hook."

"No. We worked very hard this afternoon. His problems aren't horrendous. Teller is willing to work. I told him he was lucky he can speak clearly, that you had to work long and hard to overcome your lisp."

"Then you just let it slip?"

"No, I wanted Teller to know how hard you had had to work. I remember. I remember the frustration and the irritation when your *s* wouldn't sound right to your ear. How you had to stop and do the sound again. You really worked hard, and you should be proud of yourself. Teller was impressed.''

''Not for long. He's needling me.''

''Ah, but he's always been on the receiving end of gibes. Be patient. He admires you.''

''Yeah.'' The word was scornful.

''I know kids and there's—''

''You're not much more than a kid yourself. But you say that you know them? You've left me open to Teller's scorn.''

''I've left it open for you to show him how to cope with his own problems. You succeeded. Your success will be a goal for him.''

He sighed tiredly. ''I took it all those years ago, I can take a little more. I won't be around long enough—''

''Where are you going?''

''Somewhere.'' He said the *s* deliberately and looked at Jo.

''You're not staying here?''

''Hell, no.'' He looked down as he shifted his feet. ''I worked too hard to get away from this nosy, closed little town.''

''Then...you're not going to stay here and go to bed with me?''

His head snapped up and his stare bored into her.

She turned out her hands and looked so innocent. ''In the play,'' she explained.

''You're a witch,'' he accused.

''Watch how you pronounce that.'' Then she said, ''You'll have to excuse me. I must get dressed for the party.''

"What party?" He scowled at her.

"At Mrs. Carstairs's house. Aren't you going? Everyone's invited."

"Mrs. Carstairs?"

"She's celebrating her first hundred miles." She looked at his puzzled face. "Her new car," she explained. "The red one."

"She's only gone a hundred miles?"

"I think she carries it on her back most of the time so it won't get dirty."

"I'll come by and pick you up. I don't like going into parties by myself." He gave her a blaming look but it had been he who had spent the afternoon on the phone. "By now, everyone in town is remembering that I once lisped, and I'll have a hell of a time at the party. You have to help me be brave. If I don't hit anyone, you have to give me a kiss."

When he said "hit," Jo had automatically lifted and smoothed her hand to the back of her hip. His soul cringed with guilt. He said, "May I escort you to the party?"

"Okay. But hurry up. I'm hungry."

"This is just for a drink, isn't it?"

"You're taking me to the Pizza Place afterward. Protecting shy people from slurs and snorts gives me a voracious appetite." She treated him as if he was younger than she and not too socially bright.

When he came back for her, he drove into her drive and knocked on the kitchen door.

She took a little time getting there but she opened the locked door and said, "You're supposed to come to the front door."

"But you always go in and out of your back door."

"You're still slow."

Bob didn't understand that remark but he wasn't curious enough to ask what she meant. He took her coat and held it for her, frowning at her. "Is that what you're going to wear?"

"Obviously."

"Where's the top to that skirt?"

She frowned back at him, then looked down at her dress and said, "I am perfectly decent."

"You may be, but that dress isn't. Why don't you go change? We have time."

"I'm wearing this."

"Well . . ." He sighed deeply. "It's been a long time since I had any challenges."

At Mrs. Carstairs's party, it seemed inordinately odd how many people had trouble with their *s*'s. Bob smiled at the clumsy needling and was tolerant.

Felicia noted who was nudging her son and gave them her "look," which could wither steel at twenty feet. She came to stand by Bob and ask his tormentors about very personal and embarrassing gaffs in her marvelously penetrating, carrying voice.

Bob suggested, "Leave it, Mother, I'm a big boy now."

And Felicia said, "We Browns stand together. I remember your brave indignation when That Man in Cleveland gave me a mediocre review for *Anthony and Cleopatra.*"

"He was wrong. I saw the play. You were magnificent."

"Yes." She smiled at her eldest. "So are you, Bob. In so many ways. Don't let these gnats annoy you."

"They aren't." He smiled at his mother and suddenly realized it was true. He was no longer pricked by the needles of sly teasings. Why was that? He looked into the clear liquid of his drink as if into a crystal ball. He'd been through so much worse things since that long-ago time of lisping, that the nettles of goading by the people of his childhood were friendly teasings.

He excused himself from his mother's group and went in search of Jo. She was surrounded by men. Bob was irritated by that. But as he watched, she stepped back, left the group and went into the kitchen. Bob followed.

She glanced up and commented, "No one has attacked me as yet."

"Do you expect to be attacked?" He frowned at her.

"You implied it would happen," she told him as she replenished the hors d'oeuvres on the plate in her hand.

He hadn't noticed she was helping Mrs. Carstairs, and he hadn't seen her carry in the depleted serving plates. "Don't lean over."

She gave him a surprised look. "Why would I do that?"

He was studying the ceiling and brought his gaze down to her. "If you need something off the floor or need to reach across the table, let me get it for you."

With her back straight, she leaned over, looking at her chest. Her dress stayed in place. She said, "It doesn't gap."

"Put your arms forward as if you're setting a plate on the table."

She did that, her dress gaped, and Bob sucked in a shocked breath.

She mentioned, "You seem very informed about the necks of women's dresses."

"I've made a study."

"I can see that you have. Why?" And she had the gall to stand there expecting a reply.

"So that I can tell them if their dresses gap?"

"How noble of you."

He consulted the contents of his drink. "It's good that you understand. There could be people who would mistake my diligence." He lifted his bland face.

And she laughed.

He decided right then that they would practice getting into bed.

Mrs. Carstairs came hurrying in. "Bob!" she exclaimed. "I haven't told you how much I love that little red car. It zips around without my permission. I simply go along for the ride. I went in to Cleveland yesterday and got some of the hors d'oeuvres, and I was back before I knew it. Thank you for finding it for me." Then hesitantly, she asked, "What did you do... with my old car? Should I know?"

"It went to that motor heaven beyond the sunset."

"That's lovely. I'll remember that. Here, dear, carry these in, will you?"

So Bob carried two plates into the dining room. He turned to watch as Jo brought in two plates. She gave him a snippy look, bent her knees and put the plates on the table without a gap. He grinned at her. And she laughed.

They went to the Pizza Place and they were a little mellow. She asked if he'd collected the eggs that day.

"I have to do it tomorrow. Why don't you come and help me?"

"You still have to do chores?"

"As long as I live there, I have to do my share. Everyone does his share."

"As long as you live there. Where do you intend to go?"

"I'm restructuring my goals and redefining my needs."

"You're going to become a bum."

"I thought I might volunteer for the forest service."

"Why?"

"Remember the spotted owl out west? There are other creatures who need woods. Think of the rain forests that are being burned off in South America. I want to plant some trees."

"You can do that here."

"No land. None available for what I want."

"I have ten acres. Want to plant some trees there?"

"Ten acres? Where'd you get those?"

"Remember Mrs. Ahern? She was such an interesting woman. I loved her rocks and went rock-hunting with her. I watched her polish them and cut them and make things from them. From her father, she had ten acres outside of town. After she died, I found she'd willed the land to me. I'm not sure what to do with it."

"What's on it now?"

"Now much. Some weeds, a 'sink' that's marshy, some scraggly trees. No buildings."

"Not even a shed?"

"No. We used to go out and tramp around and look at all the variety of wild flowers and weeds. Those were such great times. She knew a name for everything."

"She studied plants?"

"I'm not sure. She might not have been right about the names. How was I to know?"

He grinned as he shared her humor. Then he said, "I was thinking about you on my way back from your house this afternoon. It shouldn't have surprised me that you're interested in theater." He gestured. "Since you are interested in it, I can see why you want people to be able to understand the language."

"Yes. I have a double major in education and theater. It took me an extra year to finish. I knew I'd come back here and the theater group is strong. I wanted to be involved. It's people who interest me. Communication. Even being of the same race and tongue, people *still* have trouble getting their ideas across. You can see how important it is now that we communicate with peoples who are different and who don't speak our language. It is astonishing how an idea can be so diversely interpreted."

"You should hear how a board meeting goes." He shook his head. Then he qualified the statement. "In a board meeting that is really open and not controlled by one man."

She guessed, "That's what you've seen. A board that was controlled."

"Not at first."

"What happened?" she asked, watching him.

He didn't look back. He said too casually, "A new man came into the business."

"It was he who took control?"

"Yes."

"Were his ideas sound?"

"Reckless."

"Why didn't the rest of you stop him?"

"He had the boss's ear." And more, he had the boss's daughter's attention.

"What happened?"

"I protested. I was fired."

She chewed the bite and studied Bob. "I think you made a lucky escape."

Those were Salty's words. Bob's smile was ironic. He shook his head a little, not in denial, but in ruefulness.

They drove to her place, and Bob saw her to the door. He took her key, unlocked the door and allowed her to enter first as he said, "You owe me a kiss."

"Why?"

"I fed you supper."

"I'll sing for it." She took off her coat and got a slouch hat and a cane from the coat closet. She did a basic sand shuffle, singing "Show me the way to go home—" She jiggled inadvertently as she strutted and tipped the hat and moved the cane around. It was a routine she'd learned at some time. "I'm tired and I want to go to bed—"

Bob said, "Okay."

She waggled her head over the "—drink an hour ago—" and lifted inquiring eyebrows.

"The practice for our part in the play."

"You silly. Go home."

"I get a kiss." He watched her soberly, his head down a little, his interested eyes on her.

She went on with the practiced routine, singing "—to my nervous system—"

"A kiss."

"—firma, H-2-0—"

"Now."

"I have to fin—"

He moved to her and took her into his arms and kissed her. There was silence. She dropped the cane with a ringing clatter, and her hat fell off; but as the kiss continued, her hands crept up to his head and she made sounds of savoring.

It wasn't only her hands that lifted the hair off his head. His whole body went into some kind of intense shock. Then his arms tightened and the kiss got really serious.

As he became more rigid and began to tremble, her body loosened and her bones sagged. But her mouth was greedy under his hungry demand.

He broke the kiss and pulled his head back so that he could stare at her in his stupefaction. His arms didn't loosen, but his look almost accused her of something. It was even a little indignant.

It was wasted on her. Her eyelids were heavy, her mouth was soft and making little movements that made his nerves shiver erotically. He almost kissed her again, but his stern upbringing interfered. He loosened his iron embrace and was almost sundered by her small sound of protest.

Gradually he released her, steadying her, being sure that she could stand alone, and he moved back from her almost an entire foot measure.

That kiss! What had happened to kissing since he'd last been kissed... over a year ago? Longer. He was stunned as he watched her thrilling need to recuperate and her gradual struggle to regain control.

He'd done that to her.

At what cost to himself? Would he ever be able to be even briefly idle without reliving this encounter? What in the world had just happened to have caused such an erotic collision of senses?

It had been too long.

Yeah.

He'd lost . . . touch . . . with the sensual side of himself. But what about her? She was young and free. She had no excuse to react to him with such outrageous abandon. She hadn't even tried to resist him! She'd just cuddled up and put her body up along his and she'd—

Bob took a deep breath and walked stiffly around in odd, uncalculated circles and rubbed his hand on his chest and breathed some more, trying to distract himself.

The trouble was that he couldn't see and his mind was swamped with electric thrills. So was his body. Maybe it started with his body and that swamped his mind with all those images of what he wanted. Needed. Craved.

He put a bracing hand on the doorjamb and slid a supposedly casual-looking hand into his trouser pocket, but with his equilibrium chancy, he didn't cross one foot over. He stayed with both feet reasonably planted and braced, with that hand on the doorjamb.

She had both hands on the kitchen table and her arms were straight. Her head hung down and it seemed all that held her up were her braced arms. Slowly she looked up through her messed-up red hair and she said in a croak, "You ought to wear a warning sign."

That just about did it. He shivered with need. He panted, unable to really get any oxygen so that he felt as if he was suffocating.

All of that really very brief sampling was proof that he could be susceptible to redheaded women. Or worse, specifically to Josephine Malone.

He hadn't worked as hard as he had in order to get out of tiny, enclosed Temple, Ohio, to get so entan-

gled with a redheaded woman that he'd be trapped
there for the rest of his life. Thinking of the conse-
quences sobered Bob. Sobered. She had intoxicated
him with just a kiss. He recognized the trap. Any
smart animal, once caught, does understand traps and
only stupid ones get caught a second time.

He said, "Thank you for a very pleasant evening."
He smiled to soften his rejection. "See you at rehearsal."

She watched him walk steadily to the door—how'd
he manage that?—open it and leave.

He drove home, then got out and walked around the
Brown property until he felt that he could relax and
sleep. He'd made a very very narrow escape.

Five

———

Halloween came and in a town the size of Temple, it was planned for and anticipated with practiced calculation. They had a nighttime Callithumpian Parade. Anyone in the town who wanted to, dressed up in some kind of costume and marched in the parade.

Bob had almost forgotten what it was like. And nostalgic memories of other years came back to him. It was odd to be in the place of his childhood and remember the child and the young man he once had been. With a good will, Bob helped in the preparations, remembering odd events, pleasures, and other people who were no longer living in Temple.

But Bob found he was judging those still there. Their involvement, their contentment. The support they gave each other. And that was underlined in the way his billing/bookkeeping business was growing.

For the coming Holiday, nature helped with the decorations. The trees were in their spectacular autumn dress. But the townspeople, too, decorated Temple two weeks in advance. They contrived cornstalk scarecrows and fat, carved pumpkins and gathered the prerequisite spiney bittersweet, a fence row vine with orange and yellow berries. Bunches of it were for sale for winter bouquets. It all took a lot of time and planning.

Just about everybody in the town pitched in and worked at the food preparations. It was a prodigious undertaking, but it was good for the community. And so many people were involved that for a whole week, Bob found it fairly simple to avoid the trap who was Josephine Malone.

People from all around the area attended the festivities on Halloween. It was an Event, and the town raked in a very nice profit for their Community Center by selling pumpkin pies and cookies and bread. They made and sold taffy, the sinful caramel-covered tart apples on a stick, hot dogs, and sloppy joes. They had root beer and lemonade available, and—best of all—parking spaces for the strangers's cars...for a fee.

The parade was the drawing card. People love being in parades. The non-townspeople paid a small fee to participate. Nicely spaced between the marchers were bands from little towns around Temple and some were from Cleveland.

Bob didn't march with the costumed Brown household. He didn't dress in costume for the Event. And for the parade, he deliberately stayed alone, finding a place along the curb among strangers from out of town. He watched the marchers, recognizing old friends, mostly now in family groups. He was reminded how many of his old buddies were settled family men and had growing children.

Whole families walked together in the parade dressed alike as skeletons or clowns or ghosts. And kids laughed and cried and shrieked bloody murder. And just about everyone had a great time.

Afterward, there was a dance at the Community Center with an admission charge and more food supplied by the town for sale.

Bob went. He went "to see old friends," he thought, and was irritated with himself. In the three months he'd been home, he'd seen every living soul in that small town of less than three thousand. Actually, he finally admitted to himself, he went to the dance to see if Jo would be there and who had partnered her.

She came with a bunch of witches, and she, too, was dressed as one. She looked a lot like the TV spook lady Elvira whose clothes weren't quite on her, and Bob was scandalized! He was so aghast at the sight of her that he pushed through the crowd toward her to put his shirt on her. Then he saw that most of the costume was skin-colored material.

He was so close, by then, that he had to speak to her. She was sober-faced and nervous with him. And some guy took hold of her arm and tugged her away. She kept her eyes on Bob. He knew she did because he was watching her every minute to see if she paid any attention to the guy. She did dance with whoever it was, but she turned her head and peeked at Bob.

He left soon after that because he knew he shouldn't interfere in her life. He did realize that. He needed to get away from Temple and make his life someplace else. He couldn't stay around the temptation of Josephine Malone. He could louse up her life. And maybe his.

He walked home conscious of being a solitary figure, by himself in the night, in the dark, leaving behind the town's glow of light. Back there, everyone else was laughing and calling and talking. Only he was alone. He sighed. His life wasn't what he'd planned it to be. Here he was, thirty years old and he was back to ground zero.

It was better that way. He couldn't get entangled with Jo and cause her to miss him when he left. There weren't that many single men around Temple for a woman her age. But then he remembered the crowd of men around those witches. That clear picture slowed and stopped his footsteps. He turned back and looked toward the noisy, celebrating town and he almost went back and claimed her.

But he did resist. He needed to protect her from himself.

The next day, the citizens of Temple went to the cemeteries in one of their mass clean-up visits during the year. Almost all of them had been there to tidy up and put flags on the graves for the Fourth of July. Now they cleared the late summer's accumulation of grass and weeds and put flowers on the graves of their kin and friends.

The Browns were there, all of them, and Bob was reminded how long Felicia's people had peopled that place. This place held half of his roots. And they went deep. Being there at that time was an important reminder of how long his people had striven to hold and keep a place during terrible times and hard times, but mostly with good times. Temple was his home...his native land.

* * *

In the following days, Bob hadn't actually talked to Jo again. He had managed not to "see" her at a distance, and had altered his destination when he knew she would be along his way.

He was no longer concerned with protecting her. He realized he had been protecting himself from the woman trap of specific allure. He recognized that she was dangerous to his freedom. And that freedom was all he had. He would never again give it up by putting it into the hands of a woman.

But unobserved, he observed her; and he could feel the pull of her on him. He could have relinquished being Papa in the play, but he had never confronted Porter.

However, after Mrs. Carstairs's party for her new car, Bob had removed Papa's kiss for Mama from the scripts. That was a last-minute alteration. He'd re-typed the script page, photocopied it for the rest of the scripts and re-stapled the pages. Neither Salty nor Felicia mentioned the change.

Bob knew that Salty was coaching Teller in his role as the lead reindeer. Then Salty had included another two kids, and those three had taught the other five. Finally all eight were prancing and pawing reindeer. Salty had cleverly integrated and coagulated the group. Teller was comfortable with the other reindeer, and they had accepted Teller well enough.

Bob told his dad, "You were smart to do that for Teller."

Salty dismissed any praise. "He's a good kid." He looked at Bob. "He listens when you speak."

"He's waiting for the lisp."

"I think he's impressed that you don't."

"Teller?" And Bob made a disbelieving sound. Then he asked, "Who's going to be Santa? You?"

"With this voice? You jest. I'd sound like a cigar-smoking Al Capone playing Santa."

Bob grinned and said, "What a great idea. Have the sleigh bells be the sounds of old whiskey bottles hitting together. The 'children' would be mobsters. Instead of mice, have rats."

"Who would be Mama and Papa?"

"Mae West and W.C. Fields?"

And Salty gave his rasping chuckle.

Bob asked again, "Who will be Santa?"

"Well, none of the perfectly rounded men wanted it. So we settled on . . . Porter."

Bob's face went from a frown, as he considered the man, to gradually clearing amazement and he said, "By George, I think you've got it! He'll be perfect for it." Bob was impressed. "It's a good thing I wanted to be Papa—" But he hadn't. It was only that he'd been in a corner and he hadn't been able to slide out of it. "I'm glad you were able to find Porter a role."

They had the first general reading. The groups gathered, the narrator read and the various little people did their practiced parts. It really went quite well. Teller's eyes sparkled and he didn't go off into the wings when the reindeer were idle.

But Bob had trouble. The "bed" was a too narrow table with two pillows close together. He didn't want to lie down beside Jo because he was so conscious of her and her delectable, inflammatory body, that he was afraid he might embarrass himself.

Since he'd put the questions to Jo, he felt he had to say them to Felicia who was the director. Everyone listened. "How do I get into bed?"

They all laughed. The kids especially, since everybody knew how to get into bed. Bob smiled and was patient.

Felicia said, "You'll be wearing a nightshirt, not pajamas, and you'll have a red nightcap on your head. You will see the children all nestled ... the sugarplums ... but not the mice. The mice will see you as you walk by their niches.

"Jo will be in a high-necked, old-fashioned nightgown with long sleeves, and she'll be wearing a ruffled cap. As you see, the bed is not important to the reading, and it will be tucked back into that recess.

"When you get into bed for your long winter's nap, you will lift the covers from the audience side, sit on the bed and swing your feet under the covers. You will lie down on your side and put your hand under your cheek and close your eyes. Let's try it."

As he checked the kids and fireplace, Bob's pacing was wrong. Felicia was brilliant. She slowed him until he really paid attention. He must have done it a half dozen times. Then he went over to get into bed.

He was agonizingly aware of Jo lying on the table that was too narrow.

Felicia looked at her son thoughtfully, then she said in her most gentle voice, "There is no need for the rest of us to stay. Practice awhile. Get it smoother. Act as if you are married and the kids and house and the Holiday are yours. Jo, give him some direction."

In various rustlings and quick exchanges of words, all the rest of the cast and help departed. Salty said, "Be sure to turn out the lights." And Bob's parents left.

The last door banged shut and there was silence. Dead silence.

Jo lay on the table. Bob stood, abandoned. With the stage lights dimmed to nighttime, and only the table-bed with a spotlight, Bob's features were cast into a mask with the light on his head and shoulders, his forearms and down his body to his sex and thighs. He looked at Jo and said into the silence, "Who gave you permission to wear that witch's costume? Were you flaunting yourself?"

She relaxed, sighed in an explosion of impatience and looked disgusted.

He walked over to the table and put his hands on "his" side of that "bed." "Do you know what you do to me lying there on your back?"

"Good grief, Papa, control yourself. The kids are in the next room!"

"How do I get into bed?"

"Back to that? You lift the sheet and sit down, then you swing your feet under the sheet and lie down. It's no exhaustive trick."

He sat on the table next to her hip, lifted the sheet, and swung his feet up and under the sheet. But as he pulled the sheet over him, his body continued the turn until he loomed above Jo, with his weight braced on one elbow.

They looked at each other very seriously. Her red hair was carelessly tumbled like living silk on the pillow. Her eyes were green jewels. Her lashes were a dark rust color like her eyebrows. Other than a chicken pox scar above her left eyebrow, her skin was flawless and pale. Her mouth was soft. He said, "Whoever heard of a redheaded witch?" The he lowered his head, and he kissed her.

It was a serious kiss that lasted as he tasted her mouth. He moved his free right hand up under her sweater and under her shirt. She wore no bra, and his hand hesitated as the thrill of her slithered through his body. Then his hand curled around that flattened mound, and he worked it so that it rolled in his hand. And he kneaded her with leisurely sensuous pleasure.

She freed her mouth and said, "Cut that out."

But she didn't push him away.

He waited, watching her, his mouth smiled just the tinest bit and his lashes closed almost entirely. He could feel his feet turn into a goat man's cloven hooves, and horns sprout. He could even feel a tail begin to grow. He said, "Touch me."

"I don't think so." Her lips had some trouble forming those sassy-sounding words, but she did shake her head just a tremor. Her gaze never left him and the green of her eyes darkened.

He took her unresisting hand and put it under his sweatshirt, sliding it over his hairy chest. He shivered with the feel of her captured hand.

"Are you cold?"

"No." He had to clear his throat. "I've wanted your hands on me."

"You've avoided me. You didn't even dance with me at the Center on Halloween."

"If I'd stayed, I'd have made you wear my shirt."

"I wasn't cold. There were too many people around. The place was packed and you—"

"You looked half-naked," he scolded as he moved his hand on her breast.

"Well, you have to know I wasn't. I wouldn't have worn that dress as it looked. Why didn't you stay and dance with me?"

"I'm not staying in Temple."

"What does that have to do with anything?"

"I don't want to get involved here."

She looked up into his eyes and opened her mouth to reply, but he kissed her again for a long squishy time and her knees became restless.

He turned her toward him and slid his hand down her back to her bottom, which he turned so that she was pressed against him. She groaned, and he smiled wickedly and his hot eyes glowed.

He moved to undo the top of his jeans when the outside door clanged open and footsteps echoed in the lobby.

He got off that table, buttoning the top button of his jeans and straightening the sheet in one fluid motion.

She gasped, "You've done that before!"

"What?"

"You've been caught in bed with some forbidden woman before!"

"No," he said distractedly.

"Then how did you know to do that so quickly and so perfectly?"

"My dad was a sailor."

She blinked over that as the theater door opened and Porter stood there and said, "Ho, ho, ho."

Bob turned his head dangerously and was about to snarl, when Porter said, "I couldn't get here sooner. Did the children perform perfectly? Why are you two still here?"

Bob realized the fake laugh had been Porter's Santa entrance. Bob had his hands thrust deeply into his pants pockets. He turned slowly and said, "I'm having trouble...pacing."

"I know. If we don't do this right, the whole thing will be over in ten minutes."

Jo curled up and leaned on one elbow. "Some things—" she said "—need more time."

Bob glanced at her, and she gave him a bland, serene look. She was telling him he needed time to make up his mind. Bob considered that. Hadn't he decided to leave? Or did he just think he should?

Porter had been two years behind Bob in school. He was not quite as tall, but he was tousle-haired, a little plump and his round face was very cheery. "I'm excited to be in the play. I've always been a spear-carrier." That was the label of anyone who did walk-ons. Porter smiled. "Felicia asked me to be Santa last May. I can hardly wait to play a real part."

Ah, thought Bob, so Felicia's dramatic surprise over Bob's agreement to be Papa had been a fraud! Porter was never slated to be Papa. Bob made conversation. "Getting down the chimney should be interesting."

"Haven't you told him?" Porter smiled expectantly at Jo.

"I don't believe so."

He explained to Bob, "They don't actually expect me to come down the chimney. I'll just jump a couple of feet from a platform in back of the chimney facade."

"Ahh," said Bob as if he'd been spending good time mulling over that problem.

Porter paced casually back and forth, looking very possessively around the stage.

Bob knew there was no way that Porter would leave until they did. He glanced over at the still-reclining Jo. "Do you have your car?"

"No."

"Come along. I'll walk you home."

"No need." Porter held up a delaying hand. "That would be out of your way, but her house is right on mine. I'll see her home."

What does an allegedly disinterested man say then? "Well, I'll see you both at the next rehearsal." He gave Jo a blank look. Then he went over and picked up his jacket. He found that he hesitated. He told himself to get going, he'd been stupid enough for one night, and he left.

But on his way home, Bob asked himself if he *was* leaving, why wasn't he sending out résumés?

Thanksgiving came, and the absent Browns and the various harbored ones all descended onto the household. Several were home from college and among those was Salty and Felicia's own youngest, Carol, who was a lifetime friend of Jo's. The big, sprawling place was almost full. Of course, Georgia and Luke were there. It was a madhouse.

As much to get away from all the noise as anything else, he thought, Bob went to Jo's. Her family was home. Her brother John was glad to see Bob and sat and talked to him. Her mother said hello and narrowed her eyes at him. Obviously, she knew Bob might leave Temple and she wanted to discourage him from hanging around her daughter.

John's children were polite and quiet. A sharp contrast to the offspring of the various and diverse bunch at the Browns. With the three Malone children so organized and controlled, Bob decided Mrs. Malone was a terror. Another good reason to stay clear of her daughter Josephine. Mrs. Malone should know that she had nothing to worry about from Bob Brown who had been permanently cured of women.

Two days after the swarm of locusts who were relatives and adopted kin had left, Bob came back to the house for lunch to find Salty and Felicia sitting at the kitchen table with Felicia holding a wet cloth to her forehead.

"What's the matter?" Bob inquired.

"She's going to be fifty." Salty's rasp was tender.

Dramatically, Felicia's lower register said, "I'd completely forgotten." She lifted the cloth away and her eyes were enormous and dark. "Fifty."

"I told her it's no big deal." Salty was gentle and smiled a little.

"How like a man to say something like that." Felicia discarded her husband.

"I remember fifty." His rasp was a little miffed.

"You're a man."

"I'd noticed that," he said.

Felicia petitioned Bob. "How can I survive—here—and face another birthday with everyone...knowing?"

Bob was practical. "Where would you like to be?"

"New York."

And Salty said instantly, "We'll go. Bob's here. He can handle anything."

"Wait a minute." Bob held up both hands and turned his head to one side.

Felicia wasn't deterred. In her tremoring basso profundo, she said, "You'd deny me leaving?"

With her tone, Bob could hear the clang of caging bars crash down around his mother. He squinted his eyes and considered her. She was really very good. "Go. I can handle anything."

"See?" the Rasp said to his fragile Wilting Flower. "I knew we could count on Bob."

With some harsh irony, Bob said, "I lost my job and wife just so that I could save you from spending your fiftieth birthday in Temple."

Her voice shivering with delicate emotion, Felicia said, "How thoughtful."

Bob warned, "Don't push."

By happenstance, Bob found they already had their reservations and even had the tickets to the plays that Felicia wanted to see. Tickets for plays had to be reserved months in advance.

Then he walked into the lower hall later to find his parents standing there, and he heard, "If you insist, I'll take the mink." Felicia was deciding. "It's gaudy to flaunt it here. It will be a treat to wear it, darling." And she stretched her hand out toward Salty so that he could take it and lift her fingers to his lips.

Disgusted, Bob wondered why God had saddled him with those two. What awful hams.

He counted noses at supper and asked if everyone was present? There were only five responsibilities there. Twelve-year-old Teller never ate with the rest of the family. But there were the two little girls, both age six. "I think I ought to call Georgia or maybe Terry to come stay, too."

"Jo's coming out."

"What!" And Bob was startled to find his body so alarmed. Alarmed? It wasn't that, it was *excited!* He looked into a mental pit of degradation. He was going to have that tempting Josephine right in his own house with his mother and father away in New York!

His mother was explaining. "Jo Malone. She's coming to stay with the girls."

"She can stay here—unchaperoned?" He felt the need to have it on record that he had made a query.

His mother would scoff, saying that in these times, there was no problem.

His mother said, "No, of course not, dear." Felicia was patient and concerned he hadn't understood. "Mrs. Thomas is staying over, too."

"Good grief!" Bob was appalled.

"That's what Jo said."

"When was that?"

"When we told her we were going to New York and asked her to stay with the girls and suggested Mrs. Thomas as chaperone."

"Before you finagled me." A statement.

"You were somewhere or the other, and we couldn't find you."

"Hunting eggs?" Bob was being sarcastic.

That amused his father.

Then Bob frowned. "What about the play?"

"Jo will direct from her bed on stage."

"How long do you intend being in New York?" His voice was a little strident.

"A while. We aren't entirely sure. Until I feel that no one here will remember that I've...had that birthday."

After that, there was a flurry of preparation getting the pair ready and arranging for the various activities that they were involved with to be put off onto other volunteers. Bob found the whole damned town had known before he had, that he and Jo would be sitters for the six—alone—with Mrs. Thomas.

Temple's citizens were avidly interested. The women's eyes sparkled and the males just laughed out loud. Not a couth one in the bunch.

So Jo moved out to the Brown house. Bob and the boys helped with her things. "How long do you intend staying?" Bob inquired with the second trip up the stairs to his sister Georgia's old room with Jo's things.

"Who knows?"

And Bob had scowled. The reason he scowled was that his body was celebrating. He would have time to devise some way of satisfying his need for this woman. Purge this unexplainable, riveting interest. He looked on her and felt—possessive? Surely not.

Mrs. Thomas was driven to the Browns' by Porter. The tiny, bony, dark-wigged, nosy old lady was ushered inside and up to the parents' room.

With Mrs. Thomas upstairs, settling in, the other adults sat in the sunroom, waiting to depart for the Cleveland airport.

Bob had been surprised by his parents allowing anyone to stay in their sanctuary. He commented on just that very thing. "I can't understand you allowing that old biddy to stay in your room."

The parents shared a smug look. "Well, darling," his mother purred. "She would get in there anyway, you have to know that. So we've removed some things...and—" her voice deepened wickedly "—we've planted a few others."

Placidly, Salty added, "Felicia has shot our reputations all to hell."

"Not at all." Her voice lightened in studied offense. "I've merely given her something to think about."

Salty was positive. "The whole town will guess that you've duped her."

"She won't." Felicia smiled and blinked her eyes like a spoiled cat.

No longer interested and content to allow the conversation to continue to veil the fact, Bob sat sprawled back in his chair and slitted his eyes so that no one would guess he was studying Josephine Malone. That red hair of hers looked like the perfect counterpoint to the house. It was as if the house had waited for her to come inside for it to be complete. How could that be? What would a house care who lived in it?

With Mrs. Thomas there for the children, Jo went along to the airport to send off Felicia and Salty. The senior Browns kissed her fondly and hugged Bob. "We'll be back in time for the play. No question. We know it will be brilliant."

The pair leaving smiled in benediction, waved a last time and disappeared down the flexible tube to their plane.

The two left in the waiting area did linger until the plane closed its door, taxied away, and disappeared into the distance. Planes took off, but the watchers had no idea which takeoff was heading to New York.

They left the terminal, took a tram across to their particular parking area, found Bob's car and began their drive back to Temple.

Bob looked at his watch. "It's late. We'll never get home tonight. We might just as well get a room at a motel down the highway and stay there."

From the corner of his eye he saw the slow turn of her head. Her voice was patient. "From the motel to your parents' house is five miles."

"That's a long way to travel."

"We'll be brave. Mrs. Thomas will be up, sitting by the light in the window, guiding us to our beds."

She'd made the beds plural. Bob wondered how long his parents planned to be gone. How much time did he have?

And he considered his thought. He was definitely planning to seduce Josephine Malone? Wasn't he going to be careful of her feelings? Well, she was a grown woman. She knew about him. He'd warned her.

He was going to seduce her. With six kids and Mrs. Thomas cluttering up the place, how was he going to do that?

There had to be a way.

Six

——

Bob didn't sleep well that night. Just down the hall, past Mrs. Thomas, was that delectable Josephine who was probably sleeping the sleep of false innocence. Bob directed his guardian angel to go into her room and plant lascivious thoughts in that redhead. His guardian ignored him.

Then Bob tried to think how long it had been since he'd been this distracted by a female body. Years. He hadn't had a fever like this since...since he was about fifteen. And he recalled his restlessness and Salty seeing to it that he had a great deal of physical exercise.

He got out of bed, put on jogging clothes and a cap, then quietly went out and down the steps, through the house to the porch. Outside, he began warming-up exercises. He jogged to town and through it, and did the town's perimeter, waking the dogs along the way.

Between their distanced selves, the dogs had to discuss the fact that some nut was out running loose around town. That made people open windows and hush the dogs. In about a half hour, Bob had managed to waken just about the entire town's canine and adult population.

On his second circuit, the sheriff's car eased up alongside Bob and said, "You've picked a hell of a time to jog. What's bothering you?" And Jim Varner laughed, har-har-har.

Bob stood with his hands on his hips, dripping sweat on that cold night. He knew full well that Jim knew Jo was at the Brown house. Jim was referring to frustration. Bob couldn't allow anyone to believe that he had a teen-age sex mentality. He said, "Jim, this is a free country."

"You're disturbing the peace and feeling of security that is the right of all dogs and citizens."

"Are you sure it's my jogging that's doing that? You ought to look around. After all the strangers that came here for the Callithumpian Parade, some crook must think the rake-off the Temple citizens made must be around somewhere. Why don't you leave innocent citizens alone and watch for the crooks?"

"You shoulda been a lawyer."

"No. A plumber."

"Yeah. Do you know what Nick took for doing one little bitty pipe under the basement floor? I can't tell you because it would make you throw up and the street department would get mad."

"If I stand here any longer, my sweat is going to become ice. I would be frozen here and Bill Piper, over there, would come out in the morning for his paper and find me. He'd have a heart attack and you'd be sued.''

"Under those circumstances, maybe you'd best trot on home.'' And he laughed real dirty.

Followed by the sounds of hostile dogs and slamming windows, Bob continued home. However, he wasn't tired enough so he ran up and down the lane a couple of times before he figured maybe he could sleep.

He went up the front porch steps and opened the front door. There he was confronted by Mrs. Thomas wielding a rolling pin! She swung, and Bob leaped aside in the nick of time. She screamed, "Awk!"

And he yelled, "Mrs. Thomas! It's me!"

But by then the Brown dogs were barking, everyone else in the house was awake, and even the cats were coming downstairs.

There were unsurprising inquiries as to what was going on? And one of those seven people on the stairs was Josephine. Her hair was down around her shoulders and she had on a soft purple robe. Purple!

It looked great. She stared at him calmly. She replied to the kids' questions. Saul at sixteen had a sympathetic look that irritated Bob. Jo sent the kids off to bed and came down the stairs to ease Mrs. Thomas into a chair.

Mrs. Thomas was having spasms of gasping and excitement. She'd confronted the burglar and vanquished him.

Bob took off his hooded sweatshirt and growled at Mrs. Thomas. "It's me. Bob."

"I," corrected Mrs. Thomas.

"Yeah." He thought the old biddy had admitted to being hysterical.

Mrs. Thomas recovered really quite rapidly as she lectured, "You're supposed to say, 'It is I.'"

"Okay. Are you all right?"

"I heard you running in the driveway, and came downstairs. Then you came up on the porch!"

Jo patted her hand and said, "You were very brave."

"I was terrified, but I had the responsibility of those children—" And she put a hand to her forehead.

Bob watched that through narrowed eyes. It was a very Felicia-like gesture. Mrs. Thomas, however, could not match Felicia's voice. Bob wondered if sleeping in Felicia's bed had tainted Mrs. Thomas with Felicia's bent to dramatics? And he wondered how soon his parents would return.

Then he looked at Josephine Malone, kneeling in a puddle of purple robe beside Mrs. Thomas's chair. Jo's hair had been tumbled by her sleeping. She looked delectable, and Bob immediately wiped out his mental demand that his parents return. He could tolerate Mrs. Thomas until he'd sated his lusts in Jo.

His body shivered at the very idea of doing that.

Jo said, "You're chilled."

He nodded. One always agrees with a woman when her ideas can be used. She now needed to take a page from *The Outlaw* and Jane Russell's Good Samaritan gesture and take him to bed to warm him. He waited.

She said, "I'll fix you some cocoa."

Cocoa! Cocoa?

Mrs. Thomas said, "None for me."

Bless her heart!

"I need to get back to my bed."

She was probably sleeping on Salty's side and having lascivious dreams about old gravel voice. He helped Mrs. Thomas up the stairs. "I'm sorry I scared you."

"It's a grave responsibility to care for six children."

"Yes. It is. But you have us to help with it."

She slid a glance over at Bob as if that wasn't much of a comfort. She said dryly, "Don't keep Josephine up long. She's tired."

"I'll get her to bed as soon as I can." He said that with an earnest face.

She gave him an uncertain glance.

"Felicia has nerve pills that soothe her. Let me get you one. They are completely harmless. Over the counter."

He fetched one from the hall bath with a cup of water, and he watched her take it. He smiled and relaxed. "There," he said.

"Don't go out running again."

"I won't."

After Mrs. Thomas closed the door of his parents' room, Bob checked on the little kids. They were already drowsy and languid. Those kids could handle anything.

As he shut the last door, he became aware of the fact that he was standing in sweat-dampened clothing . . . and he probably smelled that way.

Would it be too obvious if he showered? It would take too long. She'd give up, leave the cocoa on the stove and go back to bed.

He went to his room, ripping off the covering layers of clothing, and put on his pajamas. Without a robe, he went barefoot down the stairs and into the kitchen. It was a little chilly.

But he caught Jo about to leave the kitchen.

"I thought you'd gone to sleep."

"I gave Mrs. Thomas a sleeping pill." He looked at his watch.

"Why?"

He shrugged innocently and said blandly, "She had an upset. She needs her sleep."

"Oh. Do you have another one? I can't sleep."

She couldn't sleep? Her tumbled hair was from . . . restlessness? "Do you need to jog, too?"

"Maybe so."

"We'll have to do it earlier," he said, watching her pour the cocoa into a cup and add marshmallows. "You're supposed to put the marshmallows in first."

"Really?"

"In these years, the Browns have made an intensive study of cocoa. You always put the marshmallows in first."

"Sorry."

"It's okay. You're still young enough to learn." And he could teach her all sorts of things. He wondered if she would sit on his lap. He smiled at her. "Come, sit down and talk to me."

She hesitated, but she did eventually get to the table and she did sit down, but she sat on a chair. "About what?"

He'd forgotten. "What?"

"What did you want to talk about? Not still hung up on getting into bed, are you?"

"Funny that you should mention that. I've had it on my mind."

She slid a careful glance his way.

For a woman only twenty-three, she seemed reasonably aware of the nuances of conversation. But she didn't giggle or flirt. One of the cats jumped up on his lap. Why couldn't she do that? He asked Jo, "Who've you dated? Anyone steadily? Lived with anyone? Going with anyone now?"

"Lived with anyone? In this town? With Mrs. Thomas just next door? You are funny."

"You didn't kiss me good-night. It upset me so that I had to go out and jog in order to settle down."

"Ha."

He frowned. "You're not supposed to say 'Ha!' over something that serious. It's in the rules that we all kiss good-night. Didn't you notice that I gave the girls each a kiss and the littlest boy?" Jake was eleven.

"Nothing was said about your kissing me."

"Well, of course, they had to leave in a hurry and they couldn't think of everything. You have to realize that." He put the cat on the floor.

She smiled, almost. "I'll remember tomorrow."

"You need to kiss me, tonight."

"I'm not sure that would be wise."

"Why not?" He was astounded by her hesitation and opened his arms out to show how ordinary it would be. The cat jumped back on his lap.

Jo reminded Bob, "You're not staying in Temple."

"Now, what would that have to do with anything?" She'd once said those same words.

"I might become ensnared."

He shook his head slowly, elaborately side to side. He explained as if it was old instruction, "It's just practice. It isn't ensnaring. You have to keep in practice in case someone comes along that you want to kiss and—" he put the cat back on the floor "—if you weren't practiced, you could botch it."

"How clever of you to think of that."

"I'm out of practice." He confessed, a little elaborately casual about it. "Except for that one mind-boggling kiss you gave me in your kitchen, and the stage one, I've forgotten how to kiss a woman."

"I don't believe we should exchange any more kisses like those."

The cat jumped up on Bob's lap again, and he again put it on the floor. "Oh, but there're other kinds. There are friendly ones, ones of affection."

She was cautious; he was selling.

"Just one little good-night kiss isn't going to deplete your supply. I'm needy."

She was wavering.

"The cocoa was delicious. Thank you." He took his cup quickly to the sink to rinse it and got back in time to help her out of the chair. That was slick.

As she stood up, he prayed that her nose was clogged so that she couldn't smell him. He put his arms around her and kissed her exactly as he'd done in her kitchen.

It was just the same. His brain melted and sloshed around, his arms trembled, his knees locked to keep him erect. And he was certainly erect.

He broke the kiss, and they clung to each other, panting. He hugged her to him and groaned, gasping. "I thought you were only going to give me a friendly one."

She replied, "Hmm?"

So he kissed her again the same way.

In the middle of the kiss, Bob heard someone on the stairs. The most vital part of his brain, automatic reflex, was still operating, and he reached out and turned off the kitchen light.

Teller's voice called, "Jo?"

Bob said, "Coming."

Jo said, "Hmm?"

"It's Teller, looking for you."

"Teller?"

She was in worse shape than he! Bob smiled. This wasn't going to be at all difficult. He hugged her tightly to him, then turned her and guided her to the doorway, sending her out into the back hallway.

Teller saw her and asked, "What are you doing?"

And Jo said, "Hmm."

In the dark kitchen, Bob smiled like the goat man he was. He listened to the two go up the stairs and their footsteps faded. Then Bob was left alone with just his needy body.

He couldn't go out and jog again, so he went upstairs, dressed in outdoor clothing and went outside, set a lighted kerosene lamp on a stump and began to split up logs for the fireplace. The dogs came over companionably and watched.

He'd done about three log sections when he heard a rather strident voice say "—Bob!" And he realized immediately that it hadn't been the first time she'd called.

He looked up at Jo, hanging out of the girls' winter-screenless window. He grinned and went over under it to say, "Juliet, thou art fair as the morning light."

In some snide response, his flower retorted, "Will you quit chopping that wood? What's the matter with you?"

He opened his mouth to tell her but it was then he noticed that four of the kids were at the windows, looking down soberly at the madman who was chopping wood in the middle of the night. Saul and Ben watched tolerantly. So Bob only inquired, "Mrs. Thomas still asleep?"

His Beauty didn't reply but questioned, "Do you do this often?"

"Only recently."

"You have the entire household awake."

Again, he asked, "Mrs. Thomas, too?"

"No."

"I wouldn't think so." He smiled a little ruefully thinking of the wasted pill.

The dogs turned their heads from one to the other with interest.

"Will you be quiet so that we can all sleep?"

"Naturally." Then he said, "Anyone else hungry?"

Kids are always hungry. And a midnight snack was a treat. So there was a chorus of agreement. He'd expected that.

This time the cats beat everyone to the kitchen and they got their expected bowls of milk to shut them up. The kids helped with glasses and milk and did the toast, and Jo was impatient with Bob. He whispered, "It's all your fault. The jogging and the wood-chopping. You have to know you could solve me very easily."

She gave him a puzzled frown.

She didn't understand? She thought he was really crazy instead of simply going that way from unsated lust? Could she be . . . an innocent?

In this day and time? Naw.

She continued to watch him, trying to figure him out, and he just waited. But she shook her head, a little impatient with him, and fed the kids cinnamon toast and plain milk. No chocolate for them at that time of night.

Knowing kids, Bob didn't make any conversation. Jo was silent. Replete, the cats left the kitchen to find their favorite spots. And the kids began to yawn but they lingered.

Bob had sat in the daddy chair, so he could just reach backward and turn out the overhead light. He said quietly, "Put your dishes in the dishwasher."

Obediently, they began to get up to do that. The girls first, then the big boys and Jake. Bob had to nudge Teller. Then Bob realized that Teller had been sitting there at the table with them just like everybody else. This had to be a first. So Bob said to a trailing along Teller, "Will you see to it that the girls are in their rooms okay?"

"Yeah."

"Good night, Teller."

"Yeah."

Jo said, "Good night, Teller."

He smiled back at Jo. "Yeah."

Jo was straightening the kitchen. Bob got up and wiped the counters and the table. They heard the doors close upstairs. He said to her, "Teller was down here with us. He didn't take his food somewhere else."

"He's coming along very well. Have you let him look at a motor lately?"

"Have you?"

"He uses more patience. It surprises him. He said, 'This wire goes in here!' He hadn't bothered to really pay attention before."

"He's never again mentioned that I lisped. Only that first time to let me know he already knew and didn't have to do anything to find out."

"It was important that he know."

"Could it be that you're smarter than I?"

"Ahh," she said and smiled. "Even you begin to learn."

"Why, you sassy woman!" And he swatted her backside.

She turned back toward him and gave him a waiting look, and he realized what he'd done. He said softly, "I meant to tease you, I'm not a man who beats people who are smaller or weaker than I."

"I know that."

"Did you all along?"

"Not that first time. But with Teller right there, I understood later why you had floundered so awkwardly. You actually won points when you couldn't betray the fact that you'd thought I was he."

"Salty has been working with Teller for the play. He showed him what to do, then allowed Teller to be the one who taught two other of the reindeer and those three then showed the other five. Doing that made it easy for Teller to feel important and accepted. Simple. It was brilliant."

"He gives little clues to how his life has been. In understanding why something happened. He doesn't know his parents. He was abandoned. He feels—left out—left over—alone."

"I don't see how he could in this house."

"He hasn't been here long enough, yet. Your parents are remarkable people, Bob."

"I understand that, but I accept it as normal because I grew up in the middle of their expanded love. It's normal for them to gather children into their house and love them in a wonderfully offhand, hands-off caring. If I ever have children, I'm going to leave the kids on their doorstep."

"They wouldn't mind that, but you'd be so curious that you'd move in, too, in order to watch the kids grow up."

He grinned, then he looked around in an assessing manner. "Well, it's a big house. They won't notice I'm here, too."

"What about your wife?"

"We are divorced, we had no—"

"No, not her. What about the mother of your children? Wouldn't she be curious about them, too?"

Expansively, he gestured at the interior of that house. "There's plenty of room. She can move in, too."

"You imply that she wouldn't be in your room. Do you intend to just go around giving women children and then coming home, your goal completed?"

"That sounds like a *great* idea! The only trouble is, after a time, Salty would start nudging me to contribute to the household expenses."

"My mother wants me to buy our house from her. I can't until I'm hired full time. But I do have the time to tutor the kids who need help."

"Your mother ought to move back here. If John had the full care of the kids, he would hussle around and get himself another wife."

"—or a series of bad baby-sitters."

"That sounds like Auntie Jo. You have to know that your mother is interfering with the natural progression of lives."

With irony, she suggested, "He should apply for welfare and Aid to Dependent Children and stay home and take care of the kids himself?"

"Why not?"

"Who did this job on you that you don't want to go back out into the world?"

Bob studied her, but he didn't open up to her yet. He could not. He replied, "I'm working for Men's Liberation." He started lightly enough. "The way I have it figured is that men have carried the burden all these centuries, fighting animals that wanted to eat the little wife and kiddies, fighting other men who wanted the little wife or some of the kiddies, and fighting wars that greedy old men start and everyone knows are totally stupid. And in these enlightened years, we men have continued the battles, fighting for jobs, for promotions, for the little wife and kiddies' safe and secure and comfortable lives. We get on the treadmill with stress and long hours. We kill ourselves in these new battles. It's time for the women to take over. They've always known how to do everything better. Let them try."

The silence in the kitchen almost had a sound. Then very softly, Jo said, "Wow."

"That's it? Just . . . wow?"

"She must have been a real bitch."

And he realized that, again, he had said more than he'd intended. He was embarrassed to have so clearly betrayed his bitterness. He lifted his hands and opened them out in a very poignant gesture. Then he dropped them to his sides and said, "It's late."

She waited for a minute, almost expectantly, then she said, "Good night, Bob. Sleep well." And her voice was very gentle. Thoughtful. She waited another minute, then turned and quietly left the room.

Jo had been waiting to be kissed. Bob understood that. But after that speech, he could not have kissed her gently. Therefore, he could not kiss her. That puzzled him. But he did understand the kinds of kisses. It truly was as he'd told Jo. There were all kinds of kisses. And some of them were the kind that communicated even hate. He'd had that kind, but it had taken him a while to recognize it was so.

He went up the stairs and checked the kids, then he went to his old room and sat on the bed. He wished that Jo was lying there, and he could lay his head on her soft breasts and give way to his battered and shredded emotions.

Why would Jo want to comfort him? She didn't even know him very well. Outside the fact that they had shared some spectacular kisses that had really rattled both of them, why would she want to give him surcease? To heal the wounds given him by another woman? No.

He thought of his ex-wife. Deliberately remembering her. He'd shut the reality of her out of his mind, hidden it. And finally, he "saw" her for the first time as she really was, as she had been all along. Actually, it was a relief to admit what she was and to be away from her. That was an odd thought. Relief? If that was true, then why did he hurt? Why did he feel . . . wounded? His trust had been betrayed.

He lay down and pulled the comforter over him. He yawned and stretched and took pleasure in the moves. How long since he'd yawned and stretched that way? It was a little like his stomach growling that time. Were these signals that he could revive his pleasure for living again? Well, his lust had certainly revived. He wanted Josephine. He smiled into the night. And he just might actually get her. She'd waited for a kiss.

What if he actually could coax her into willingness? Umm. To have her in his bed and willing?

He began math problems. He stuck to them with determination and he finally went to sleep.

Salty and Felicia called and said they were fine and having a marvelous time. It hadn't snowed in New York.

They'd had almost a foot of snow in Temple. The kids loved it. Bob got to put the blade on the tractor and plow the lane so the kids could get to the school bus.

The rehearsals would soon be twice a week. The play would be on Christmas Eve. Bob learned to get into bed with Jo and could handle doing that well enough. But there were other things beside the play that would have to be done.

The gift shopping had taken place all year long and presents were hidden, but the cookies had to be baked, the fruitcakes made, nuts cracked and separated. The house had to be decorated and the tree chosen. And with the first week of December, they had St. Nicholas's Day to celebrate.

When a child arrived to live with the Browns, each was given a wooden shoe with his or her name painted on it. It showed they belonged to the family. It was a symbol. And on the night of the fifth of December, the children put their shoes in the hall by their bedroom doors. Then on the morning of the sixth, St. Nicholas's Day, they found a gift in their shoe. It was tradition.

This year it was Bob who doled out those gifts, and Jo put a sprig of holly and some walnuts in each shoe.

"No coal or switches?" she asked.

Bob shook his head. "We take the positive approach."

Continuing with her knitting, Mrs. Thomas asked, "Who was Dutch or German in your family?"

"Some on both sides. You have to notice how pragmatic mother is."

And Mrs. Thomas giggled.

Mrs. Thomas?

That skinny old lady had surprised them by being an excellent cook. She loved seeing the kids clean their plates. Bob served the children small helpings so that they could ask for more, and Mrs. Thomas would beam.

When Salty and Felicia called, the kids would say, "We're saving you a gingerbread man!"

And Felicia would ask Bob, "What is that woman doing to Salty's reputation as a perfect cook?"

Bob would reply slyly, "Challenging it?"

So the house was filled with hustle and bustle and secrets and giggling and the insidious aroma of gingerbread, cinnamon and nutmeg.

Seven

In those early days of December, Bob was fairly busy at the car lot with the laggards who were late getting their cars winterized, and those who were having their vehicles checked over or tires switched for a Holiday trip.

The billing venture was going very well. Mary Swanson was an organizer and kept things neat, filed and orderly, while Vincent Harding was an excellent accountant. There were times when Bob wondered if Salty had sorted them out early in the summer, before Bob had ever known he was coming home?

The weather was crisp and cold. A new snow made everything look as it should for that time of year.

The little kids brought home colorful and eccentric pictures of Santas and Christmas trees and Holiday poems. Those had to be hung in windows or on doors so that everyone could see them, and the collection became part of the decorations. It had always been done that way in the Brown household.

Bob had very little time alone with Jo. They talked constantly. He came home from work, she greeted him, and not kissing her was not natural. They discussed their days, and Mrs. Thomas had comments. The kids would listen during the meals and have their own contributions to the conversations. Bob was almost contented, because it all seemed so natural. This was how it had been when he grew up. Lots of people, lots of opinions.

He realized he'd been lonely for a long time.

But there were snatched times when he waylaid Jo in halls and had straining, foot-shuffling killer kisses that had to be followed by open-mouthed breathing to soften their panting. And he sneaked his hands around, checking her for feminine traits, but she didn't allow much of that.

Anything is solvable. Bob found that he had to go to the attic and find the house and tree decorations. Of course. Jo would help with that, up there in the attic was a clumsy four-poster.

At the car lot, Bob arranged to go home to see what would be needed for the coming Holiday decorations. That way, he would contrive to make his arrival appear an apparent impulse. He knew that was the day Mrs. Thomas would be at the Community Center, at her club's Christmas party and playing bridge. She would be gone the entire afternoon.

Jo would be home.

He'd looked on her appointment calendar and seen that she had nothing scheduled for the day. So she would be home alone. A perfect time to—uh—check things out. And he smiled.

Bob cheerily went home and opened the door from the foyer into the big lower hall to call, "Hello!"

Two little voices replied! He went to the door of the living room to see the two little girls before the fireplace, cuddled in blankets and reading. They were glad to see Bob. It took a long, long couple of seconds for his mouth to stretch into an answering smile.

Jo came along and said, "Well, this is a surprise."

He thought she'd understated it. He kept his mouth stretched. "Colds?"

"Stomachaches. They're okay."

"Need anything done?" He had nothing to say and so chose to offer help.

She shook her head. "What are you doing home?"

"Uh. I need to check the tree lights."

Jo smiled. "Good thinking. You know, there are some fir trees on the Ahern land that I inherited. We could cut a tree there. The kids could go along and all the dogs. We could have a snow picnic and it would be different."

"We could go look, first." Bob had been on tree-cutting expeditions. Every kid militantly chose a tree and the arguments were endless. Salty had always thought it was good practice in debate. Bob, however, knew to plan ahead.

"That's a good idea. When would it be convenient for you?"

"Whenever you're free." They could take the van, he thought quickly, scrabbling for ideas. He *had* ideas. Lots.

So he went to the attic. Fortunately, the Navy-trained Salty had been the one who had controlled the storage. Everything was clean, labeled and easily found from a master list on the attic door. Bob did get to sort through the boxes of ornaments and check the lights to see if they would work. Some did.

December was a busy time. The rehearsals at the Community Center were going so brilliantly that everyone was sure their performance would be a flop. Even the littlest kids knew the poem by heart and they were all getting tired of that, too. One night, they all joined in, saying the words along with the narrator. As the director, Jo understood the varying moods of performers and she tolerated that scrambled evening's conduct. There were so many giggles and gaffs that the practice was a hilarious shambles.

Then on another day, with the roads freshly plowed from a new six-inch snow, Bob had to take some files home to check them against Salty's records. He had to leave his car at the head of the lane because the snow had drifted. He walked in with some delay, but he had on boots. He stomped up the cleared steps and across the porch to open the door. He shed his coat and boots and stepped inside...and Jo was home. There she was, home! So was Mrs. Thomas.

Stymied from having a close encounter of the nth kind, Bob changed his clothes. Jo had tea and cookies for him, which he ate and sipped, standing up and watching her pack cookies in tins to give as Christmas gifts to neighbors and friends of the Browns. They spoke in a desultory manner. Her cheeks were pink, he supposed from the heat of the oven. Then he went out to plow the lane clear so that, after school, the kids could walk from the school bus to the house more easily.

When he'd put the tractor in the shed and returned to the house, Mrs. Thomas said, "No one gathered the eggs this morning. I need some eggs."

Bob's breath stopped for an electrified second. Then he said with great care, "I could do that, but the hens aren't penned, you remember. It'll take a while. Is that okay?"

Mrs. Thomas frowned at Bob and said, "Well, I don't need them, really, not until this afternoon."

Bob explained with great candor, "They'll be all over the barn. Jo, why don't you come along and help?"

She was busily distracted as she was now sorting through recipes at the kitchen table. She looked up and said, "Okay." She went for her coat and boots.

So he got her out to the barn.

He threw a little grain into the straw on the floor of the barn and the chickens gathered, clucking, scratching in the straw and making sounds as they busily pecked for the grain. The cow shifted and swished her tail and the unridable pony went outside.

Bob took the basket down from its nail and handed it to Jo. They began hunting. Bob was very diligent and feverish to get the egg-hunting over. He put the eggs where Jo could find them easily. The basket already held quite a few when he took her up to the loft and, sure enough, there were some nests up there.

With those nests emptied, Bob took the basket from Jo and set it carefully aside. "I'm starving for one of your whammying kisses."

She looked around the loft. She'd played in that barn since she could walk home with Carol. She was familiar with every aspect of it, and knew all the animals very well. She asked, "How'd I get up here?"

"It's your competitive instincts." He soothed. "You wanted to find the most eggs." He tugged her down on the straw. She didn't resist, but she didn't help too much, either. He sat her down and then kissed her, leaning her back until she was lying partly under him on the soft straw. She cooperated.

The kiss was that very same kind, addling their wits and ruining their nervous systems, disrupting their heartbeats and malfunctioning their breathing. Utter chaos.

But he fought against the paralyzing effect and heroically managed to make his trembling fingers unzip and unbutton and become more intimate. He was clever in sliding fingers under and around and finding what he sought.

And she was shifting minutely to help make his maneuverings easier when the door banged open and footsteps entered the barn. Jo gasped and, being on top, Bob kissed her, swallowing the gasp before he slid his mouth to her ear and breathed his hot hot breath into it as he warned, "She's down there."

He didn't lie. It was the back door that had been opened, and there was no shoveled path into the snow for Mrs. Thomas to trod to that door. It was the nanny goat. "She won't come up the ladder." He promised. That, too, was true. The ladder was perpendicular. "Just be very still."

Jo lay unmoving as Bob then held her prisoner to silence. His tongue explored her ear quite thoroughly, making her nipples peak and starting all sorts of interesting sensations touching through intimate parts inside her.

He kissed along her chin and discovered her mouth. He sampled ways of enjoying that portion of her, and he gave her the deep kisses that filled his soul with rapture. Her breathing became sporadic, and she was swooning.

With the occasional footsteps of the goat below, covering little sounds, Bob moved clothing craftily aside and moved his mouth on Jo. And when she stiffened in erotic response, he misunderstood and gave her another of the double-whammy, surefire, woman-stunning kisses.

Under the sound of the goat nibbling at the pony halters, making them rattle, Bob donned the condom. Jo gasped, and he had to pretend alarm, his hand to her mouth, his head lifted to "see" if "she" was coming up the ladder. Then he kissed Jo again and soothed her here and there, before he whispered with hot hot breaths into her ear. "She'll hear you." With the "she," he meant the nanny goat, of course.

After a time, as expected, the goat walked over to the door and butted it open and went out. And with the sound, Bob eased onto Jo's opening body and hesitated. She could decline. But her arms came up around him and she groaned, lifting her hips to him. So he guided himself past materials and pushed-aside clothing, and he found the place he wanted, the place he longed to be.

She helped, clutching, moving, and he gasped with the amazing thrills. He slowly sank into his sheath and shivered with passion. He said, "Oh, Jo..."

And she gasped. "Bob..."

He shuddered but didn't move. "Are you okay?"

She nodded quickly, making a rustling sound in the straw. "I want more."

His breath whooshed out and he drew in another quickly to say, "Yes." The word was unsteady with his need as his body trembled.

He withdrew a little, and she clutched at him. "No!" she whispered.

He replied, "It's okay." And he pushed back into her.

She said, "Ahh."

Then he made love to her. Drums should have rolled and cymbals clashed and waves should have dashed against a pile of rocks. It was fantastic. And they shuddered to collapse. It wasn't the greatest technique, but it was very satisfying. And he knew that she was a novice.

He was sweating. He licked the salted drops from his upper lip and nuzzled his face into her hair. "My God, Jo. I've never experienced anything so wonderful."

"Bob." Innovatively, she simply sighed his name and murmured agreeing sounds.

He lifted his head and looked at her so gently. There were tears along her eyes and his finger gently wiped them away. "Are you all right?"

"Wonderful." She used his word.

"I wish I wasn't so drained—" he grinned down at her "—so that I could do it again with you."

"Don't leave me. I like the feel of you."

His wife had never said that to him, and the words were a balm to his wounded feeling of self-worth.

They lay, still coupled, kissing gently, murmuring. Finally, he said, "We need to take the eggs inside."

"Yes."

They separated carefully. He put the used condom in his handkerchief and tucked it into his pocket. He tidied his clothing and helped her to arrange hers more neatly. Then he carried the basket, and they went down the ladder.

Jo said, really quite prosaically, "Mrs. Thomas will wonder why we weren't here when she came in." And she watched him.

He was rather elaborately surprised. "Mrs. Thomas? It wasn't *Mrs. Thomas,* it was the nanny goat."

"Oh?" She raised her eyebrows.

"Did you think it was Mrs. Thomas?"

Jo said in an instructing manner, "She opened the door and walked across the floor. You said she wouldn't come up the ladder."

"She didn't. I've never seen a nanny goat climb a ladder that steep."

"You had your wily way with me."

"You're wonderful."

She suggested, "Any woman would have served the same purpose."

"Now, why would you say that? I've wanted you and courted you, and you've driven me wild. Why do you think I've been splitting logs and jogging and shoveling snow and going out of my mind?"

"You're a sexaholic?"

"Only with you," he said very soberly. "I've never felt this way with any other woman's kiss. I've never wanted any other woman's body as I've wanted yours. This wasn't just sex, Jo. You have to know that. We made love." And he looked startled.

"You act as if that surprises you." She mentioned that with interest.

He was brushing straw out of her hair. "It does. I thought I was through with women."

"Not lately." Her droll voice held some amusement.

"Oh, Jo, don't regret what we just shared. You can't be sorry?"

"No. I've always been curious, and more so lately."

"What do you mean?"

"I've allowed you a good many liberties because I wanted them."

"This was your first time? How have you managed that?"

She gave him a patient look. "I hadn't done it with anyone. I have the reputation of being cold. I go places with a gang of women who are like me. We're not easy to..." She stopped speaking.

He looked around to see why she'd stopped but no one was there so he asked, "What?"

"Well, I guess it just took the right man to show me that I am...easy."

"Just...easy? Don't you...like me...just a little?"

She looked up at him and blushed. "I'm not sure. I certainly do like to kiss you and—" she gestured to the loft "—and that was really...wonderful."

"You know it was very special."

"It certainly was. You are terrific. How did you manage with all our clothes? Have you been in very many lofts?"

"Well-l-l. I tried the first time when I was fourteen, and I'd barely gotten Be—a girl up there when Salty came into the barn. We lay up there, in rigid terror, waiting to be found out, but Salty finally left. By then, the thrill had evaporated, and we escaped."

"Who was she?"

He grinned at Jo's curiosity. "A lost chance to discover what life was all about."

"You lecher." But her voice was mild and soft. She reached her hand up and began to pick the straw from his hair and the shoulders of his coat.

He turned around for her to check his back, and when she said, "I think that's all," he turned back and carefully put his hands to her coat-covered waist. She held still for it and lifted her mouth. He put his arms around her and hugged her very sweetly. "Ah, Jo." Then he kissed her in a very gentle way. It was the first non-inflammatory kiss they'd shared and it was very sweet.

They almost forgot the egg basket and that seemed unusually funny to them. So they arrived back at the house a bit tousled, but the wind was up and their red cheeks and mussed hair were explained by that.

The lovers had no idea how many times their glances caught and held. How soft their expressions were as they gazed at one another.

The two had lunch while Mrs. Thomas watched and rocked as she knitted. After they'd tidied the kitchen, Jo organized lessons for her special pupils. She sat at the library table. At the desk, Bob checked the business records against Salty's file. They were aware of each other.

The little kids came hurrying in like chattering squirrels as they came home from school to drop their books and be told to pick them up. They did that without any real thought and ran upstairs to change their clothes and run out to the snow to play.

They could be heard arguing and laughing and yelling before they came inside from building a Santa snowman wearing Salty's old red scarf and a plaid cap that Bob had found for them to use.

After one of Mrs. Thomas's big suppers, the kids all did their evening chores after only several reminders. They sat at the round kitchen table and did their homework. The two little girls had none and played with their six-inch-tall rag dolls, pinning material from the rag bag on the dolls in all sorts of costumes.

Then they went to bed and to sleep, silent, contented and tired. In all that time, Teller had been right along with the rest. It was amazing to see the outcast joining the group. Like Ben and Saul, he'd sat up a little later, since he was twelve.

And when Bob told the big boys it was bedtime, Saul and Ben said "Good night" and went on upstairs. Teller put down his book and left the library.

Bob called, "Good night, Teller."

And this time Teller replied, "Night."

Bob and Jo looked at each other and raised their eyebrows as they smiled. Then Bob went over and picked up the book Teller had been reading. It was the *Arabian Nights*. The stories that told of magic and fortunes and genies who granted wishes.

Bob held the book for a minute as he remembered the dreams he'd had at twelve. He felt a nostalgia for long-ago times that he wouldn't repeat for anything. He lay the book almost exactly as Teller had left it. And he went in to sit by the fire, stir the embers and lay a couple of cut branches on them. Not enough to last very long.

Mrs. Thomas was watching one of her favorite TV shows and was completely engrossed in it. Jo wandered in and sat down by the fire. They talked of the town and of the people they knew in common. That gave them the excuse to look at each other.

They outlasted Mrs. Thomas. They moved around a little, listened for the plumbing and went into the kitchen. They left the light off and clashed together in a mad, passionate embrace that would have incinerated a less solid house. They scorched the paint on the walls. He chided her for doing that.

Jo said, "The paint was already that way. Salty is waiting for Abner to be able to work again and paint the whole house. By then, everything will need painting, and they'll have to sell one of the kids to pay for it all."

Bob asked, "Which one?"

Jo laughed. "I'm glad I don't have to choose! What darlings. What is the magic of your parents that they can be such a haven for children? How many have they raised beside their own?"

"I have to think. They had some that didn't want to stay. They did have a couple who stayed awhile until the parents could handle them again. But the others, at least a dozen, all keep in touch. This is home to them. You will be amazed by the influx of people and kids over the Holidays."

"I'll be home."

"You could share my room."

"You wicked, wicked man. How can you tempt me that way?"

He couldn't breathe. "Are you tempted?"

"Yes."

Their kisses gave the paint more stress. When they could stand it no longer, he took her down to the basement to check the furnace. He kept the cats from trailing along and put a wedge under the door to delay any company joining them for that furnace check.

He did have a condom, but first he put her against the wall and crowded her as he'd longed to do. She hissed an objection because it was an outside wall. He put his hands under her armpits and lifted her against his body as he carried her to another wall. It was an inside wall and cool enough but not as cold as the other had been.

After a careful appraisal to verify she was female, he carried her over to an old sofa and he sat down with her astride his lap. He opened her sweater and pushed the panels aside to free her breasts to his hands and mouth. And he got rid of her pants and underwear. As he rolled on the condom, he scolded her. "You wear too many clothes, do you know that?"

She countered saucily. "I've never heard that before. My mother had told me I don't wear enough. All my life I was told to go put on a sweater."

"Here. Let me help you." He lifted her again and eased her onto him.

"Well, how amazing." She wiggled her hips and made him gasp. Her knees were bent alongside his hips and her hands were free to open his shirt and to smooth along his interesting body, textured differently. Fascinating.

And his hands were free, as was his mouth. Their kisses became exquisite. Their lips were soft and touching, their tongues exploring. Their breaths picked up as their passions rose. Their hands and mouths became rougher as their hearts began to race and their breathing was harsher.

With the freedom of another place, they could become more experimental. He wrapped her legs around him as he moved forward on the cushion of the sofa, then he slowly stood up. She was impressed. "You are really strong!"

"Right now, as strung up as you've got me, I could probably do some really impossible things, like stand up from a sofa with you wrapped around me. You may never witness this phenomenon again. Always remember this and mention to me occasionally that once I did do it."

She laughed in her throat, put her head back so that her red hair spilled down her back and brushed his arms. And he kissed her throat. "You dressed in character for Halloween."

"A witch?" She was unbelieving.

"You've bewitched me."

"All I've done was to be willingly in a barn loft and sneak down into a basement with you."

"Are you willing?"

"You hadn't noticed this woman wrapped around you about as intimately as two people can get?"

"There's a *more* intimate way?" He pretended avid interest.

"You're the teacher."

"No. I know computers and cars. That's my limit." She assured him. "Believe me when I mention that you also know kissing and sex."

"I need an affidavit, with a gold seal that I can frame."

"Signed?"

"Well, of course!"

"Uh-oh. The whole town would gossip, and my pure reputation would be shot down."

He laughed deep in his throat in such a wickedly intimate way. He freed one hand and reached to loosen her heels from around him so that she slid from him, then her body slid down him until her feet touched the floor. It was very erotic.

His hands rubbed over her bare flesh and his kisses were rougher. He moved his body against hers and his big hands held her bottom still so that he could. His breaths were steamy hot and his body radiated the heat from the fires that burned in him.

Her bones became rubbery and she could hardly walk when he finally led her over to the sofa, laid her down and joined her there in the way of a man with a woman. He made delicious love with her. And as their passions raged, they clutched and gasped and wiggled and panted in their mutual struggle to slide over the rapturous heights and fall into paradise.

During their time for recovery, his big, still-trembling hand petted her hair away from her face with gentle caresses. As their breaths slowed, they smiled at each other, and their kisses were feather-soft salutes. And their hearts still thundered as he gently, gently hugged her lax body.

After a long time, they hunted down their clothes and dressed. Kissed. And finally they took the wedge from the door to go quietly up the stairs. They went around to turn off the lights, the television and check doors. Then they went upstairs to kiss, barely touching their lips, to smile at each other, and to separate to their own rooms.

From the shadows of the hall, Teller had watched them.

It was a puzzling surprise to the lovers when Teller became as difficult as he'd been when they'd first known him. They had no clue what was wrong. He glared at Bob and was angry with Jo. He refused to do any work at all and began skipping school again.

"What's the matter with Teller?" Bob asked the older boys. But they only frowned, too, and shrugged.

During a phone call, Salty suggested maybe someone had let Teller down? Had anything happened that would rattle the kid?

The lovers didn't know of anything different. It wouldn't be the absence of the parents, they'd been gone for better than a week. It couldn't be that.

"How's school? Any trouble there?"

"No," said Jo. "He was getting along really well."

"Something's bothering him. You need to find out as soon as you can before we lose all the ground we've gained. Do we need to come home?"

"No." Bob was positive. "Not yet. Give us a couple of days to see if we can handle it. I'd hate to louse up your holiday."

"It's like a honeymoon. You mother is a flirt."

"My mother!" Bob was elaborately shocked.

And Salty laughed.

Felicia wanted to know, "How's the play going, darling?"

"We all know the entire poem by heart. It's going so well, the performance will probably be a disaster."

"That proves it'll be perfect. I can hardly wait. I'm homesick."

Bob was practical. "So. Come home."

"I'm not *that* homesick." And Felicia laughed in her marvelous throaty way.

Called to the phone, each of the kids spoke to the Browns and had something to say. Teller hung back when Bob said, "Your turn."

Teller almost didn't. Then he grabbed the phone away from Bob and said, "Goodbye!" He shoved the phone back and left the room.

Salty said, "Hey. Bob? You do have a problem. Watch Teller. He could split. If he does, he'll go to Chicago."

"I'll be careful."

"You know he has a terrible crush on Jo?"

Bob was riveted. "He still does?"

"Any fool would have seen that."

"Ahh," Bob replied.

"What's that mean?"

"I believe you've nailed the problem."

"How?"

"Like Teller, so have I." But having told his father of his interest in Jo, he hadn't really told her. He smiled at her as he told his parents goodbye. And he gently hung up. Then he went looking for Teller.

Eight

Something serious is seldom solved in a day, but at least Bob had a probable handle on the cause of Teller's revolt.

Bob gathered all the residents for a family meeting, but Teller wouldn't come. Bob told about going for a tree on land that Jo owned. They discussed the gifts they'd give as a family, and they talked about the scheduling for the play calling for adjustments in their regular schedules. And with Teller in the shadows of the upper hall, Bob cautioned them to be kind to their brother, who was going through a hard time.

"People have different problems," Bob told the attentive five. "You may not remember before you came to live here, but each of you had situations that were difficult. You've settled in and are contented—"

"Now, wait a minute—" That was Saul, who always had an objection.

The other four booed and told Saul to pipe down.

Bob amended, "Mostly—contented."

Saul allowed "mostly."

The kids laughed, and Bob hoped that Teller could understand that give-and-take example. Those five had made a cohesive group.

"Teller is a fine boy. We hope he will stay here and stay part of us." Then he lifted his eyes to the stairwell and called, "Hear me, Teller?"

There was no sound at all.

When the meeting broke up, Bob searched for Teller but couldn't find him. He got the kids busy, and they all looked. Teller wasn't in the house.

Jo asked, "Did he skip?" Her eyes were filled with distress.

"I don't know."

Ben came in and said, "His boots are in his room and his big coat is still there. He couldn't go far without those."

Bob went out on the porch and the rest crowded in the doorway. It was snowing just a little, but there was no indication of footsteps toward the lane. However, there were small indentations of snow-filling footsteps toward the outbuildings. Bob considered. "He could have gone to the barn. Ben, would you get his coat and boots and bring them down?"

"Sure."

Bob got a heavy hat, a thick Hudson blanket and some doeskin mittens lined with knitted wool. He put on his own outside clothing against the evening cold, and Jo came in with a tin box.

"What's this?"

"He ate no supper at all and—"

One of the girls interrupted. "He didn't take his school lunch, either."

Bob nodded. Then he looked back at Jo and asked, "What's in it?" as he took the tin.

"Sandwiches, cookies, an apple, a jar with hot soup and milk."

"Good. Good. I hope I can find him."

The kids all began to busily get their own coats, and Jo said, "Let Bob go by himself. You can go out later, if Teller is out there."

Saul said, "I should go. I'm closer to his age. I can talk boy-to-boy with him." He grinned to indicate he didn't consider himself to still be a boy.

"Later." Jo was firm.

Saul said with an elaborate sigh, "Adults always win."

Bob said, "Cross your fingers that I do this time."

That sobered even Saul.

Ladened, Bob made the trip to the barn. But Teller was not there. Search as Bob did, he could not find the boy. And Bob's fear for Teller, alone in that cold, almost got control. He deliberately calmed himself and thought what the boy might do, where he might be. The van.

It was kept in the shed with the tractor. Bob lifted his pack and the tin, and went to the barn door to look toward the shed. He'd been so sure the kid would be in the barn, that he hadn't noticed those betraying little new snow-filled indentations had gone on toward the shed.

Bob followed them.

At the shed, Bob hesitated. Then he knocked on the door and called, "Teller?"

With the warning someone was coming, Bob then opened the door. While glancing around stretching and stooping to see better, Bob said, "We figured you'd be hungry since you missed supper. Here's your coat, hat, gloves, boots and a blanket, but we'd prefer that you sleep in your room. Come inside, it's cold out here."

There wasn't a sound.

Bob went to the van, and it was locked. Bob put the things he was carrying aside and walked around trying all the doors. They were all locked. He reached into his pocket for his keys and unlocked the driver's door. He put the key into the ignition, turned on the motor and the heater.

He looked into the back of the van, and a silent Teller was huddled there.

Bob wished for his father's words. What would his dad say to Teller in this awkward situation? Bob said softly, "We got some warm clothes for you if you really want to sit out here in the cold. And the girls and Jo fixed you a snack. You had no supper and you must be hungry. It's tough on your body to be cold *and* hungry. There's hot soup." Bob held the tin toward Teller.

Teller didn't move, but Bob saw the betraying flick of movement almost screened by Teller's eyelashes as he glanced quickly at the tin. Bob put the tin on the passenger seat. Then he piled the folded blanket and coat on the driver's seat, added the gloves and hunter's woolen hood and set the lined boots on the top.

If the kid had any balance of reasoning, he'd recognize that all the protective clothing had been provided to him by the family. They'd wanted him warm. Bob didn't mention that.

He turned off the motor. "I can't leave it run. You could be asphyxiated from the exhaust fumes." He took the key out and put it back in his pocket.

But then he said quietly, "You are important to us. We know you're upset but we aren't sure why. The other kids are worried about you. They wanted to come out to be with you. Jo is concerned that you would let your schooling lapse. She thinks you're very bright.

"Teller, you've been through a very rough twelve years. Those are past. You've proven that you can live in a family and pull your share of the load in school and sharing chores. You're a normal person. You have a good brain. You're blessed with a body that does what you want it to do, and you have solvable problems that only need some work. You can make your life what you want it to be."

There was a long silence. Bob started to reluctantly turn away and walk toward the shed door.

And the huddled boy snarled, "That's easy for you to say."

Bob looked back at Teller for a long time as he struggled to find a reply and he finally said, "Easy for me? Yeth it wath."

Teller just looked at Bob.

And Bob said, "Come inside when you want to. The door is open." Then Bob went to the shed door, opened it, went through and closed it gently. He looked up at God's House and closed his eyes in intense concentration, then he walked back to the house...alone.

Everybody was at the front door. They'd been watching through the windows and had seen Bob's approach. So they were all there. Bob had been concentrating so intensely on telling God how to do things, that he was startled by the clamor of questioning voices when he entered the foyer.

He scolded, "Get back inside! It's cold out here. You're letting all the heat out." Those were Salty's words, exactly. And Bob pulled his mouth down, mentioning to God that scolding about the heat was not the Salty words he'd asked to have put in his mouth.

No one paid any attention but asked, "Was he there?"

"In the van."

Bob wouldn't allow anyone to look out of the windows to monitor whether Teller was coming inside. He told the kids to stay in the rooms off the center hall and play games or watch TV. Saul, Ben and Jake did homework at the kitchen table. But Bob paced. Mrs. Thomas knitted, glancing around at them all.

Jo was busily sorting socks. She had raided the single sock drawer, matching up those that she could, but laying aside those truly single. She was going to make hand puppets for one of her tutoring classes.

At bedtime, Teller wasn't back in the house. Saul said logically, "I think I ought to go out and talk to Teller."

Bob looked at him. "Okay. Don't expect any replies. Don't push. Don't encourage him to leave."

Saul laughed. He walked to the foyer to put on the accoutrements of winter. They all went along like varying sizes of creatures following a piper. Saul stomped into his high lined boots, and pulled on his fleece-lined coat. He wound his Felicia hand-knitted scarf around his throat and flung it back over his shoulder just like Salty. He set his knitted and lined helmet on his head, drew on heavy mittens and he acted like an important person. His long skinny arms and legs, his narrow stretching out body betrayed his youth, his manner was witness to the fact that he was already wise.

"Good luck," Bob said softly.

"I would like to suggest..." Saul paused tellingly, "...you all be out of sight in case he comes back inside with me."

"Good thinking."

Mrs. Thomas stood in the living room doorway and listened.

Saul opened the door and went out onto the porch, down the steps and crunched out to the shed, stepping in Bob's footsteps, following them, filling them.

Bob watched Saul pause at the barn door, note the tracks to see if Teller had moved to the barn before he continued to the shed.

Bob said to the silent children, "You are all worth any struggle that you may need to go through in order to grow, but don't go out to sheds in the winter. It isn't comfortable."

Now that had been a Salty saying, because the kids all agreed with heartfelt sighs and eye-rollings.

"Go read in bed." Bob suggested doing that.

Mrs. Thomas said, "You're a good man, Bob." And she appeared rather surprised.

Bob bowed his head once to acknowledge she'd complimented him.

Ben herded the kids, and Mrs. Thomas trailed after them up the stairs. They all talked, exchanging comments about Teller, while getting out of the way to make it easier for him to come inside.

Jo came to Bob and put her arms around him to lay her head on his chest. He didn't object at all but helped. She told him, "You are a good man. What did you say to him?"

He told her all of it that he could remember, and he told her about using the lisp.

"You are also brilliant."

"I wish to God that Salty was here to handle this. Do you suppose your damned redheaded beauty is the basis of this male revolt? Just like a woman. In ancient times, men would have launched ships to get you back."

"I haven't done anything!"

"You breathe." He hugged her to hamper that talent.

"Not with you holding me that way."

He urged, "Let's go check the furnace."

"We've already done that a couple of times."

"And you have to notice that it's working just fine. We have to keep it going in this weather."

"I don't recall that you ever even touched it." She was sure. "Not once."

"You demonstrated how it should work by setting me on fire."

She shook her head. "We have to go to our rooms."

"Come to mine."

"Not this time."

Her reply about set him on his ear. He gasped. Then he had to let her go so that he could walk around for a while.

"We need to get out of sight. I'm going to make some puppets."

"Should I wait down here?" Bob asked. "With all of us vanished, don't you think he'd feel like an outcast that was being ignored? Shunned?"

"I honestly don't know," Jo admitted. "If Saul thinks we should be out of sight so that Teller can come inside in this weather, Saul might know best."

"I think I'll read the paper in the living room."

"I can see that."

"Good night, Jo."

"You're a good man."

"Having kids around is a strain."

"From what I understand, there are good things about that, too."

"I never gave my parents one minute of strain."

"You should have seen them last summer, before *you* came home. They talked about how to act, what you might need of them, what they should do, if you'd resent their interference, all those things."

"I didn't know."

"You knew to come home," Jo reminded him.

"Yeah."

She went to him and hugged him. "I'm glad you did."

"Kiss me good night."

She tilted her head and allowed that, then she said, "I need to get out of sight."

He watched her go up the stairs, then he went into the living room and sat by the fireplace. He put some more logs on, replaced the screen, and settled down for as long as it would take for at least Saul to get back.

What if Saul decided they should both split? Saul had a key to the van. Would he agree to take off with Teller? Saul had been a Brown member for how long now? Since he was four? Twelve years? Would he be entrenched enough to stay? Hell, how could anyone know? Even kids that had lived at home with their parents, all their lives, would take off. Even being a genetic member of a family didn't guarantee commitment.

Think of all the problems people had that didn't concern anything other than just not getting along together. Bob shook the paper and sighed. He went on pretending to read as his mind sorted along all the things that people found difficult that hadn't anything to do with food or shelter but almost entirely hinged on personalities. Their prejudices had nothing to do with differences in beliefs, status or race because the kids were generally from the same families. It was a puzzle.

So splits in non-family families shouldn't be a surprise. Yet, it was always a surprise of complete disbelief. Unacceptable.

Sound carries particularly well with a blanket of snow. Bob heard the shed door open—and close— then footsteps crunched in the snow. Bob's intent ears distinguished that they were those of only one person. He felt a great letdown. He folded the paper and put it aside, still unread. Then he got up tiredly and went to the window to watch Saul's progress across the distance.

There were *two* figures! They were walking as deer walk, in their leader's prints. As Saul had used Bob's prints in going out, now Teller was using Saul's. They were laughing silently, Saul turning to watch Teller, then taking giant steps and standing to see if Teller would, too.

With relief flooding him, Bob went to the kitchen and when he heard the front door open, he began to efficiently empty the dishwasher. Saul came to the kitchen door. Bob looked up and saw that Teller was there, but back a way. They had left their outdoor clothes in the foyer.

Saul said, "We're going up now. Good night."

Bob swallowed before he replied, "Good night, you guys."

And as he absently finished emptying the dishwasher, Bob wondered if Salty had ever worried or sweated this way over any of the kids and remembered only laughter and peace. Then he thought more closely. His father had always known what to say and when to be silent and listen. He'd always been calm in times of real stress.

The only time Salty spoke in his low rasping growl was when a kid was completely out of line. But while Bob could remember that dire growl, he couldn't remember why it had been used. He only remembered that when it had been used, it was serious.

What would Salty have done tonight? Dragged Teller back to the house by the scruff of the neck? Why... his dad had done that once to *him!* Bob had forgotten that. And he stood there, remembering. How did a man know when to be silent, when to speak and when to drag someone back by the scruff of his neck?

Kids were a pain.

He banked the fire, turned out lights, checked the doors and remembered the time when the house had never been locked against intruders.

He climbed the stairs feeling dejected. He did a bed check on the little kids, then went into his room. He picked up the phone and dialed New York, got the hotel and asked for his parents' room. The phone only rang.

He put the phone back in its cradle and remembered when his parents had gotten him his own phone line. He smiled a—

A female voice whispered, "Everything okay?"

He jerked around to stare at the bed. It had been Jo's voice! "Jo?" The word was breathed.

"I've been waiting and waiting and waiting, and I became so tired that I finally had to lie down to rest."

He went to the bed in wonder and asked, "Are you really here?"

"Yes."

He had never realized he could shed clothing so quickly. He slid into bed and gasped. Then he reached and brought her to him, momentarily stunned that she would be naked. He kissed her greedily, hugging her, trying not to crush her as he growled in her ear, "Why didn't you warm my side of the bed?"

She puffed in laughing indignation.

But he just kissed her again.

She wiggled to get her mouth free, and he did allow that finally. She asked softly, "Is Teller still in the shed?"

"No. Saul brought him back."

"Thank goodness. I thought I'd have to stay awake and take him hot tea or soup or cocoa every hour."

"I'd decided to take him a sleeping bag and show him how much better it would be in the barn with the animals' heat and the hay for insulation. I find my memory of a blissful childhood has been false. I've been remembering that through the years there were some confrontations with Salty and Felicia that were . . . not gentle.''

Her whisper carried humor. "I *thought* you felt very 'at home' in the barn. You appeared very familiar with it, and I just assumed it was because you'd lured innocent maidens to the loft—egg hunting.''

"No. It was my refuge. And that's interesting to realize, because when Felicia wanted me to play Papa in *The Night before Christmas,* I refused. She told Salty that she needed me . . . and I escaped to the barn. I did realize that I'd done that before, but only tonight do I recall the turbulence they endured with me, and I'm probably avoiding knowing how rough it was for them to raise me.''

She breathed the words. "My God, Bob, you're maturing.''

"Gray-haired? I can believe it.''

"No, I was teasing. I suppose it's always stunning to realize you were a headache for your parents because you have to blame somebody and parents are so handy. But, Bob, the pain of raising children is almost always balanced by more than equal amounts of delight and pleasure. Look how the other kids worried about Teller, and how Saul volunteered to help out. Didn't that make you proud?''

She could feel him nod in agreement, then he shook his head. "People actually have kids *deliberately!*''

"I intend having a bunch.''

"I pity the man who supports you and them.''

"He'll love it. All of it.''

"I can see how he would love you.''

"Really? How is that?''

"What are you doing in my bed, stark, staring naked?''

"Uh. I thought my robe might be dusty and I didn't want to put it on your clean sheets?"

"How considerate."

She slid one arm from under the covers and petted back his hair. "I know you're exhausted. I had to hear how Teller was doing. Good night, Bob."

"Where're you going?"

"To bed."

"What an airhead," he sighed in exasperation. "You're *in* bed."

She was nice enough to chuckle, however briefly, over that; but she wiggled to get free of him, various parts of her rubbing him salaciously, making him clutch her closer. She said, "Let go."

"Do you think I'm going to do a silly thing like that? I've got you here and I'm keeping you."

"Why?"

"I'll show you."

And he certainly did, but it took a long, delicious, inventive time before she fully understood. He had to explain the differences between them, why that was so—and demonstrate exhaustively. And since there was no light, except for the snow's reflection into the room, he had to direct her hands to explain better. He held her wrists in his hands and pressed her palms against him. He was slow, he claimed, because he was reluctant and embarrassed since he was so shy. That *was* what he whispered to her.

She scoffed.

When he lifted and arranged her on top of his hot steaming body, and his hands moved on her, he said the reason he'd moved her was because she'd been ly-ing on his favorite spot. He always slept in that particular spot and he wouldn't be able to sleep anywhere else on the bed.

She didn't believe him.

"Well," he said with a shrug. "If you don't want me to go to sleep, okay." He slid her off his slick body and laid her back onto That Spot. "Of course," he told her, "I'll be wide awake and bored and who knows *what all* I might be driven to doing—" he put busy hands on her and nuzzled around "—after I've counted all the sheep as they've jumped over the fence, and they're gone, who knows where all, on the other side? I'll have to do *something*—" he demonstrated diligently. "—while the shepherds and dogs round up the sheep so that they can hop over the fence for me to count them again. See?"

"What would you do?" Her hushed words were a little blurred. She was hot and restless and her legs moved and her breaths were quick.

"Well, you can just about count on it that I'd make love to you."

"Oh."

"If you're all braced for that, I might as well get started."

"Probably."

"Let's see. How did I tell you the way I'd begin?"

She attacked him! She pushed him back and did all sorts of things to him and took advantage of him because he wasn't wearing protective clothing, and she *even* had the gall to roll on the condom and was successful the third try! How shocking.

He gasped and lay rigid. She asked why he was so stiff if he was so reluctant? He replied prissily that was from shock.

"If you're already shocked, there's no reason not to go ahead."

He said a fainting, "No." But he helped with the connection and he moved.

"Why are you moving that way?" she inquired.

"I'm trying to buck you off my innocent body."

"But you're holding me on you with your boa constrictor arms."

"You're being careless, throwing yourself around that way." He panted the words. "I don't want you pitched off onto the floor and suing the Browns for support for the rest of your life."

"How cautious."

He said pointedly, "I *did* just happen to notice that you rolled on the condom."

"Was I clumsy?"

"It was...titillating." He made the word sound wicked.

"Oh." She was appalled. "Sorry. But I didn't want you to get pregnant and coerce me into marriage."

And he laughed in hushed puffs.

She had to cover his mouth and hiss, "Sh-h-h!"

But he rolled her over under him and he made love to her. He made salacious and delicious movements, and she made little sounds that he had to swallow and they fed his starved ego.

Their bodies slithered and rubbed as they moved, and their hands sought special places to smooth and squeeze and touch. Their breaths shuddered and their hearts pounded as their mouths made their own torrid love and their tongues met in a sexually teasing dance.

But they slipped too close to the edge and slid through into tumultuous ecstasy and had to hurry to catch the starburst ride. They panted through, groaning smothered sounds with the rapture that shook them like rag dolls, before they floated on the lessening aftershocks to rest again in their bed, to lie inert, breathing through their mouths, smiling.

"Ah, Jo." His words weren't steady.

She replied, "Umm."

His shaky hand pushed her sweat-dampened hair back from her face. "Wonderful."

"Umm."

With slow effort, he managed to lift his head and look down at her. Then he lowered his mouth slowly and kissed her gently. He levered himself from her to collapse beside her. He couldn't bring himself to take his hand from her, and they went to sleep.

He wakened in the night, to find her there, and he ran his hands over her in great, stealthy pleasure, not quite wanting to disturb her. She stretched and yawned. Then she looked down her chest at him and whispered, "Just what are you doing?"

He lifted his mouth from her nipple and replied, "You're in my Spot."

"Good gravy, again?"

"You pushed me to the very *edge* of the bed! I had to get out of bed into this frigid room, stark naked, and walk all the way around to get in on the other side!"

"No!"

"Yes."

"Well, I believe I need to move out of your way."

"I would advise you not to get out of bed, it's cold out there. I will allow you to climb over me."

"How noble." She started over him and he put his arms around her. Half on and half off, she fingered an impediment. "Why are you wearing a condom?" And she waited nose to nose for his reply.

"Uh, I sleep walk?"

"No." She discarded that reason.

"When I had to go through the frigid air around the bed, I put a covering on the poor thing?"

She tried not to laugh.

"Well, as long as we're awake, we might as well use the time."

"We're going to tidy the room?"

"No."

"Eat a midnight snack?"

"No."

"I give up."

"That's what I was waiting to hear."

She whispered "help, help" a couple of times.

He grunted out the words, "I'm trying, you voracious woman."

So he worked at her until he helped them both.

But then she said she couldn't stay. She'd sleep all night, and it would be morning before she wakened, and she couldn't be seen coming out of his room.

He coaxed, knowing he shouldn't. Then he kissed her goodbye until he had to find another condom.

But he finally let her get out of the bed, and he followed her, helped her with her robe, and put on his own.

"You're not coming to my room, are you? You must not."

He didn't reply but only looked at her solemnly. She stretched up and kissed his mouth, but got away from him before he could delay her. Then he stood in his doorway until she slipped quietly down the hall and into her own room.

He took off his robe, went back to his empty bed to lie there with his hands under his head, watching the ceiling and thinking. Could she love him? Could he risk trying such a serious commitment again?

Nine

Having checked the width of the front door and the height of the ceiling, Bob and Jo went out and tramped over Jo's ten acres. They had taken the van and left it in order to search. While ten acres is really a small area, for a treed ten acres, it took some time to examine the possible firs. The ceiling at the Brown house was too low. The trees were too tall.

Even with the winter bareness, the ten-acre plot wasn't unattractive. There was a meadow, a seep of glazed ice, and straggly trees, unpruned, and a good deal of deadfall. They carried manageable logs to the van to take home to be chopped up for the fireplace. Bob wasn't sure he had the energy to do that, now, and said he'd start teaching the boys how.

They did find a reasonably full fir of the right size, but it was so "stickery" that it wouldn't have been any

fun at all to handle it or to decorate it. That was dis-
appointing.

But they had promised the kids an outing and, with
the ten acres' trek in mind, Jo had the kids string
popcorn and cranberries for a bird tree in that un-
kempt area. They did extra strings for their own
Christmas tree, and several strings for a tree outside
the front windows of the Brown house so that the kids
could watch the birds eating their gifts.

The lovers did take the kids for a snow picnic. They
explored easily enough, ran and slid on the uneven
solidly frozen ice of the seep and, in the inner
meadow, they played a wild game of fox and geese on
a tromped out circle in the snow with the vital cross-
bars of escape.

Saul made a formidable fox. They all shrieked and
laughed. No one ever caught Teller, but Bob tumbled
the kids in the snow. Then Ben and Saul tumbled Bob.
He yelled, "Help! Help!" and the other kids thought
that was hilarious. They had a marvelous time. They
ate prodigiously. Every scrap.

Of course, the kids all had to see the rejected tree,
and they did agree it was too "stickery." And while it
was a disappointment not to cut their own tree, the
day had been a glorious one. They went home tired
and contented.

That evening, Jo and Bob went to a plant nursery
and bought a root-balled tree that could be planted
outside after the Holiday. It would begin the replace-
ment of the deteriorating windbreak to the north of
the Brown house. The new tree was too big to be carried home in the van, so it was delivered the next day
and set in the middle of the center hall.

The tree's branches were a little flat on one side and the top had been broken so there wasn't just a single spire. The nursery was glad to get rid of it and gave them a good price reduction and a deal for handling the planting of it after the New Year.

All the kids spent time making chains of red and green construction paper, miles and miles of it. And those were strung all over the house. In the attic boxes there were old red velvet ribbons that were wound up the stair railings. Mistletoe was hung in a doorway and the little girls giggled, but Bob stood under it and garnered kisses. "You *have* to," he'd told the girls and chased them all over as they ran giggling and squealing. And when he pretended they'd vanished and he hunted under the six-inch clearance of the bottom of the sofa or a chair, they'd run past, or rattle something to attract his attention.

It was the twentieth of December by then, and school was out for the Holidays. The tree was decorated with all the ornaments they could find, making it weighty and stunning. Some of the decorations were eccentric.

The lights all worked and twinkled on different cycles. It was awesome.

The cats had tried climbing the tree at odd times and caused a flurry among the humans, with shrieking kids and laughter and startled cats.

Bob said, "Of course, they're surprised. How many trees have they climbed with that much junk on them, with *lights?*" Then he went out to the toolshed, got some wire fencing from the barn and with the boys, solved some of the problem.

With each crisis and disturbing problem and hysterical child, Bob would look at Jo and cross his eyes.

Once she got the giggles so bad that everyone insisted on knowing what was funny? She gasped, "Bob."

The entire entourage looked at a solemn Bob and couldn't figure it out. That only convulsed Jo.

Once Jake invited the dogs in out of the cold and they had to chase the dogs down and save the cats from the tops of furniture and bookcases, and it was a madhouse. And during the scramble, Ben and Teller crashed into one another and sprawled to sit and just laugh.

Mrs. Thomas watched.

Bob said thoughtfully, "There must be a civilized way of doing all this."

"It never happened this way at *our* house," Jo said primly.

Bob nodded.

Mrs. Thomas said, quite seriously, "It's really very entertaining."

The lovers looked at one another and laughed. The kids joined in just because laughing is fun, and Mrs. Thomas smiled.

With the tree decorated, the caroling records were put on. They had hot apple cider with a stick of cinnamon, and relished squishy glazed doughnuts. For that snack, they put down sheets on the floor in front of the fire in the fireplace, and it was really all very nice.

Jo took the lampshade off one light, and hung one sheet on the wall from the portrait of Felicia. Then Jo showed the kids how to make shadows with their hands, a goose, a donkey, a swan, turning the heads and opening the shadow mouths so that the creatures seemed real.

In those next several days, wrapped presents were put under the tree and the piles were impressive. "Don't touch," everyone said to everyone else.

And at church, Teller sat next to Saul, at the other end of the pew from Bob, and he waited to leave the church with the rest of the family.

At the Community Center, the set for the play had been built on the stage. They would be able to practice the complete play as it would actually be. The kids looked at the expanse and were a little boggled.

The reindeer went up onto the housetop and one froze. He clung to the chimney and wouldn't let go. Everyone was watching. Steve's face was white. The adults were calm. Bob said, "Teller, help him."

Saul was in the chorus, and he started forward. Bob put out a hand and stopped him.

Teller looked at Steve and said, "It's okay." He studied the situation and looked around in evaluation. Then he said to Steve, "Your eyes are different." That was something Teller had just recently learned. "Look at Bob. He's not that little. See? You're not that high off the ground."

Steve's eyes moved in his frozen face and he checked that out. With Steve doing that, Bob relaxed.

Teller said down to Bob, "There's sometimes fences around the tops of old houses. We could have one, and then Steve would be okay."

Bob was amazed. "Good thinking. I'll go get something."

But the choir director said, "Let Pete. We need you here."

Saul whispered, "Put some chairs up there along the edge. It'll crowd them, but it'll help Steve."

"Very good, Saul." Then he called to the stage manager, "Saul has an idea." Then to Steve, he said, "See if it helps."

They handed low-backed chairs up and the stage manager had a fit. "What if they fall off there?"

"Only Porter and I will be down below. We'll watch out."

Everyone had remained interested, no one mocked Steve and he found the chairs helped. He was careful, placing his feet just so and watching over the side. But eventually, he was okay.

At the next rehearsal, there was a rail around the roof that looked like a widow's walk. It was just right and really added something to the visual. Especially when Jo suggested they droop cotton off the edge and paste some along the rail to indicate snow.

The kids were curious. Having practiced only in a reasonable size room, they found that they couldn't see as well because the stage was much bigger. They had to walk farther, and the narrator's voice wasn't as close.

Jo was very kind and patient. She wasn't in the bed as Mama, she was out watching and telling them how to expand and smooth their actions. She was very good.

The narrator was perfect. His voice was melodious and interesting. He handled it all with patience. He was their preacher.

During a break, Bob was standing, drinking a Pepsi soft drink when the preacher came over by him. Bob grinned and asked rather wickedly snide, "Do you really believe in Saint Nicholas?"

The preacher heaved a big sigh and grinned just a little. "Nicholas was a real person. The tree and the reindeer and sleigh were added. It's a charming tradition.''

For his own entertainment, Bob's impulse was to push, but he found that he was curious how the preacher would reply. "How do you feel about lying to the kids about Santa?"

"I don't 'like' lies of any kind. How about the Easter Bunny leaving colored eggs and the Tooth Fairy buying teeth? Why are we surprised when kids quit believing us? We lie to them all their young lives. We know those things are fantasy, but they don't. It's a hoax.''

"Why are you here, perpetrating it?"

"And you?" He smiled at Bob.

"Felicia." Bob sighed, knowing just her name was enough explanation. But he went on to add, "She told Salty that she needed me to be Papa."

"Yes. Felicia. She deals in fantasy."

"Adults can do that and know the difference, but what about the kids?"

"They, too, will learn reality. And they'll be disappointed. Then they'll do the same thing to their kids. The whole routine. Tooth Fairy, Easter Bunny and Santa and the Elves. Even the Giant Pumpkin. It's part of all the fantasies that people give to their children about the Boogeyman, and don't forget about the Goblins. Maybe it prepares the kids for adulthood, to be suspicious of anything another person tells them."

"I can accept that."

"Bob, it will warm Salty's heart when he sees Teller participating in this performance."

"They'll be coming home for the play."

"Have you missed them?"

"I suspect they left me with this mob so that I would be distracted from myself and my problems."

"And—were you distracted?"

Bob grinned. "I'd say so."

"The whole town has been concerned for you. Sympathetic and watching out for you. They were glad you came home. Do you plan to stay?"

"I just might."

"We need the young men in this town to stick around. I notice there are some, lately, who are finding Temple the place to stay. The kids getting out of college now aren't as career-oriented as the Yuppies. They are more concerned with the condition of the planet and living their own lives better. But they're still green. They need a seasoned man to help them get this town in shape. You've been out east for some time and you know the ropes of big business. You could counsel us on how to attract some selected kinds of small businesses to Temple. Like the one you've started here in billings. We have a couple of empty buildings downtown that could be used. Think—"

Jo called, "Come on, you guys. Let's try it once more."

Before they separated, the preacher took hold of Bob's arm and said quite seriously, "Let me know if I can be of any help."

Bob nodded, went past Jo and grinned at her.

She asked, "What was the serious conversation?"

"We're deluding another generation of innocent children with the fantasy of Santa."

She gasped. "Do you mean to say that it isn't true?"

He put his hand to his forehead and groaned. "Back to basics. I'll explain about fantasies later."

So later, they were in the back of the van and parked at the entrance to her land when he began to explain about fantasies. That he'd like to see her dressed in a red garter belt and black mesh hose with seams up the back, and very high-heeled shoes.

"Good grief."

"And that's all."

She huffed. "I'd catch pneumonia!"

"Well, we could wait for summer, I suppose."

"You *suppose* you can wait until then?"

He bargained. "Early spring?"

"Maybe. Are you going to be around here then?"

"More than likely. I'm courting a woman who intrigues me."

"Why?"

"I'm not sure she's a real redhead."

"That again."

"I've gotten her clothes off, but it's always been in the dark. I believe she's shy."

"Yes."

"For a shy woman, you're a barn burner. I'd hate to see— No. That's not true. If *this* is 'shy,' I can't wait to see you bold."

"You're courting . . . me?"

"You *had* to've noticed that, Jo. For Pete's sake, why do you think I keep playing around with you?"

"How?"

"Again?" He gasped. "You're voracious!"

"It's been several days since—"

"It has not! It was just the day before yesterday. And I *invited* you down to the basement *last night* to check the furnace!"

"And a whole string of kids went along plus two of the cats." She was a little indignant.

"How was I supposed to know kids are interested in furnaces?"

"Furnaces have never held any interest for me."

"Then why have you been going down there on the inspection tours with me?"

"There's a lascivious sofa that draws me."

"In ink?"

She laughed. "Ha, ha, ha."

"I really thought that was quick."

"'Quick' was when you had me against the wall that time."

"I felt like a rabbit."

"How do you feel now?"

"I don't know. Why don't you check me out?"

She worked to get material aside and buttons undone and a zipper unzipped.

He went, "Umph!"

"What's the matter?"

"Your hand's cold."

"Sorry."

A car eased up alongside and a beam of light flashed through the fogged windows over their heads.

"My God," she said. "It's Lee on night patrol."

"Oh, hell."

"What's he doing clear out here?"

A deep voice called, "Anybody in there?"

"Lee, what the hell are you doing out here?"

Lee laughed. "Nothing nearly as interesting as you!"

"Now, Lee, just a minute. You need to apologize to the lady. I'm in the middle of asking her to marry me."

"Oh. I'm sorry. Sorry, Jo."

Bob asked, "How'd you know it was Jo?"

"Who doesn't?" he called as he went back to his scout car, got in, tooted the horn and left.

Bob groused, "The whole town will know by morning."

"Know what?"

"That I've asked you."

"No, you haven't."

"You didn't hear me tell Lee that I was asking you?"

"You were telling me you wanted me to wear a red garter belt and black mesh stockings."

"Well, I've never asked any other woman to do that for me."

"I am flattered."

"Will you?"

"I'll have to see."

"You mean you're not sure?"

"I look terrible in red."

"Oh. You mean— Well, I guess you could wear a black garter belt."

She laughed.

"You knew darned good and well that I was talking about marriage. I love you, Josephine Malone."

"How can you tell?"

"I go crazy when I don't see you for just an hour or so. When it's a whole afternoon, I have withdrawal symptoms. I want you to belong to me."

"I'm a woman on my own. I don't want to be owned by a man."

"I want you to own me," he countered.

She didn't reply.

"Do you really need time to think about me, or are you being coy?"

"You have to know I'm never coy."

"I know. I was trying to get a reply."

"I'm not sure," she admitted. "How can I know if I'd be able to move away from this town, to go somewhere I don't know. You'd work and be gone, and I'd be alone. I'd have to make a new place away from all these people I've known all my life who love me and irritate me and help me."

"If I promise to stay here?"

"How can I trap you in a town this size? You've flown free for too many years."

"When I was sundered, I came home."

"Are you whole again?"

"It snuck up on me. I'm cured. And, Jo, I would like to live here with you. I want you to live with me and be my love."

"How can I know it's not just that I'm a surcease? How can I know this is a true love that will last? You told me that you'd worked all your life to get away from here and that you wouldn't stay. Then you made love with me and liked that, and now you're luring me with promises counter to what you've said before."

"Don't you love me?"

"I'm afraid to think about love. I could be devastated."

"I would never harm you," he promised Jo.

"But after a while, when you were used to me, and sexually surfeited, would you think I'd trapped you here? I want to stay here. I like this town and these people. And I love you already much too much."

"Good."

"But I need to be careful of myself," she protested. "You could wreck me."

"Oh, Jo, really and truly, I would never harm you."

"I'm the first woman you've been around since you've healed. It may be only that we have good sex. You were very needy when we began this relationship."

"I am still. I will always be with you. I love you, Jo."

"For now."

"I'd be there for you, for all of your life. Remember the storm?"

"What storm."

"When we were at the garage? And I held you on my lap and comforted you? You told me you were terrified of storms."

"That was a spur of the moment impulse. I saw an opportunity to fake it. I was just trying to get your attention."

"What? Why, Josephine, you calculating hussy!"

"And a pretty good actress. I should also tell you that I've been playing in that barn with your sister, Carol, and unnumbered others—"

"What were you doing with the unnumbered others?"

"Playing...innocently in groups. And I knew all about the goat coming in and sounding like a person."

He laughed.

She did not. She said seriously, "But when you comforted me during the storm, you said you had gotten help. That you had been afraid. How could you ever have been afraid?"

"I was. I told you the truth. I got help before coming home. In fact, she told me to come home."

"Who?"

"The counselor."

"What were you afraid of?"

"Living."

That shocked her. "You?"

"Yeah."

"Why?" she asked slowly, trying to "see" him afraid. She was baffled.

He replied quite earnestly. "I was so bitter. I had nothing left."

She scoffed. "Your life. Your health."

"That's what the counselor said."

"And . . . now?"

"She'd told me the right thing to do. In a big city, I'd been out of touch with the world. I came home to reality—and you. I love you, Josephine."

"Perhaps it's only that I allow you privileges. I was a willing woman to heal you."

He sighed dramatically. "Won't I ever know what it is to have a pliant woman? My wife wanted only her way. And it very quickly didn't include me. Would you be that way, too? I not only didn't have a loving wife but one who divorced me and got me fired from my job. And she kept everything. I have nothing to offer you but my body and my brain, my goodwill, all my efforts and my love."

Very slowly, Jo said, "You have no idea how much I want you to love me."

"Show me."

And they made the tenderest love they'd ever experienced. They steamed up all the van's windows, and they never said a word. Their touching was exquisite, their kisses gentle and sweet and their bodies loving. It was a love of another kind.

The dress rehearsal for the play was the day before Christmas Eve. Everyone was in costume and the stage was dressed for the play. The stage Christmas tree was up and decorated, the stockings were hung by the fake chimney with care, the beds had been installed for the children to nestle in and for Mama and Papa's long winter's nap. All was ready.

With the kids in costume, everything suddenly felt and looked different to the novice actors. The mice were in gray costumes and their faces were all that showed. Additionally, all the mice wore a black ball on their noses and painted whiskers on their cheeks. They carried their long tails.

The children became confused and one just stood still, looking around, and one bawled. Some were confused as to who was where, because they'd gone by faces and all the faces were changed.

Jo told the mice, "Let your tails drag. Don't worry about them. If someone steps on the tail, just wait a minute. If someone *stands* on your tail, go back and pull on the skirt or pantleg. That person will look surprised and get off your tail. Work it in that way, whatever happens.

"If one of the baby mice cries, it's okay if the real mother comes up and comforts it, then puts it back on the stage to go back into the play. This is a family performance. Don't worry about anything. But the smoother it goes, the more professional it will look. Do you understand?"

To make it easier for the littlest ones, Jo explained, "It's like your hair, a couple of strands can be out of place and you can appear fine. But if your hair's a tangled rat's nest, you look awful. Be as smooth as you can. Now, let's try it again."

They did. After that, Jo called for a rest. They sat around and discussed a summer play for the coming year. They talked about a Winnie the Pooh play, and the kids laughed and were delighted. Jo said they would check out who they needed to contact for permission and what it would entail.

Then Jo smiled at them and said, "You're all just terrific. I can't wait for tomorrow's performance. Thank you for your hard work. Sleep tight tonight. I'll see you tomorrow. Be on time."

The Browns, Jo and Mrs. Thomas went home in two cars. Saul drove Ben, Jake and Teller in one car. Jo, Bob and Teller were the only ones actually in the play. The other kids were in choruses for the singing of the carols after the play. The two little Brown girls were sure the play would be beautiful. They exclaimed over the costumes and how real it had all seemed.

When they all got into the house, the two little girls coaxed until they all stood around the tree, holding hands and sang the song from "How the Grinch Stole Christmas."

Even Teller sang.

Mrs. Thomas leaked a tear. Then she exchanged a telling look with Bob and shooed the kids up the stairs.

Jo said, "I'm tired, too. I believe I'll go on up. Goo—"

"Not yet." Bob stood with his hands in his pockets and an especially sweet look on his face.

"Some problem?"

"A proposal."

"Now, what."

He said with a head shake, "I have never met a more unromantic woman in all my life! You're supposed to get fluttery and nervous and . . . eager!"

She said soberly, "I want a stable marriage."

Bob hesitated as he considered. "Stable?" He slowly emptied his pockets and put the contents on the table under the hall mirror. He stood first on one foot and then on the other as he slid off his shoes. Then he leaned over and stood on his hands!

Jo asked, "What on earth are you doing?"

"I'm proving that I'm stable. An unstable man can't do this."

She sighed and tightened her mouth, then she sneaked a quick glance at him. He was kneeling, watching her.

She tried not to smile.

"I am, you know. I'm stable and committed. Even you have said I'm a good man. I've given you my heart. And now I have a ring for you so that everyone else will know, too."

"A ring?"

"I sold my golf clubs."

"No!"

"Well, we don't have a golf course here anyway."

Her laugh was a little watery.

He rose to his feet and went stocking-footed to the table to bring back a small, dark velvet box. He pressed the release and it opened. The ring was beautiful. It had cost more than the golf clubs. He heard her sharp intake of breath. He told his love, "I love you. Will you marry me?"

"Oh, Bob."

"What does that mean?" He was very serious.

"I've wanted you since I was six and you were thirteen." The jewels of her green eyes were splintered by her tears. "I was trying to give you time, but I was allowing you samples of me to influence you. I've loved you since before I knew what love really was."

"You ought to have mentioned it before now."

"When you left for college, I was eleven years old! How was I going to influence you then?"

"Yeah. But you finally snared me."

"I knew you'd be worth any effort when you were so sweet to me during that storm and you thought I was really afraid."

"You trembled very realistically."

"I wanted you."

He shook his head in exasperation. "All you had to do was ask."

"You'd not shown any indication that you were interested."

"I resisted you."

"You ignored me," she accused.

"Since I got home in August, I've known everything you did. I just wasn't ready then."

"And now, are you ready now?"

"Yes. Will you marry me and be my love?"

"Yes."

Their kiss was different. It was gentle and kind. How strange to share such a kiss then. No, it was perfect. Bob lifted his mouth from hers and looked at her very seriously. He took the ring from the box and put it on Jo's finger. "With this ring, I pledge to you my love. Oh, Jo. I can't begin to tell you how happy I am. I'm filled with such...joy. Does that sound very corny?"

"Perfect."

"At least you don't snort in derision."

And she knew his ex-wife had not been kind to this dear, dear man. She asked, "Uh. Do you feel secure about your role in the play?"

"Sure."

"You don't need any practice?"

"Naw. It's a snap."

"No practice . . . getting into bed?"

"Oh." His face changed. "I'd forgotten that I've been getting on the table without you there. Tell me. Are Papa and Mama friends? Would he give her a little peck of a kiss? Or would he breathe fire and attack her?"

"He'd behave like a gentleman—"

"Oh," said Bob. "One of those kind of marriages?"

"—on the stage."

And Bob hugged her tightly.

Ten

Salty and Felicia returned the next morning. They'd rented a stretch limo to meet them at the airport. It arrived at the lane with blaring horn blasts and drew up to the porch steps with some drama. The interior was crammed with poinsettias.

"Here?" The driver eyed the shabby, paint-peeling exterior.

And in her deep, Talullah Bankhead voice, Felicia replied, "Of course, darling, how do you think we afford limos? Do come in for a hot toddy."

He seized the opportunity to see inside.

Chaos reigned inside the house. Bob told the little girls, "Wait in here! It's cold outside." But he allowed the boys to go out and help with the luggage and the plants.

Two little faces were pressed to the windows and squeals could be heard even through the old-fashioned double storm windows.

The chauffeur was loaded down with plants. So was Salty, but Felicia strode up the steps in her floor-length mink with great flourish and opened the door. "Darlings!" she called as if to the highest balcony in the theater. "We're home!"

There were cries of welcome.

When the chauffeur went back to help with the rest of the luggage and the rest of the poinsettias, Felicia told Bob, "I promised the dear boy a hot toddy. He's driving, you know, so no liquor."

And Felicia managed to make each child feel singularly missed. Since she knew exactly what they'd been doing, she could ask a question of each one. "Did you make the chorus?" implying that was an honor when *all* the children who wanted to could be in it. And she put her hands on either side of Teller's face and said, "What a strong reindeer you will make. Wonderful."

With Saul, she said, "You are a treasure," and she hugged him to whisper so silently, "Thank you for bringing Teller back into the family." Who would ever believe that Felicia's voice could be adjusted to be heard by only one set of ears?

Having made his own round of greetings to the children and Bob and Jo, Salty asked Bob, "When are the rest to be here?"

"Any minute."

"Do you need the limo for anything? Anyone need fetching?" Salty inquired.

And the chauffeur sat by the fire and watched and listened, starting to rise to help.

"Everyone is taken care of, and we're all set. Smell Mrs. Thomas's turkey? She brought her friend Mrs. Gates in to help."

Salty took Mrs. Thomas's hand and smiled. "Brilliant."

And Mrs. Thomas replied, "This has been such fun, so interesting."

"We're glad you enjoyed it. We owe you a favor." He was paying her a small fortune.

Rather wistfully, Mrs. Thomas replied, "I wish you had an extra room, I'd move in."

That startled them all.

Someone took Felicia's mink and lay it on the newel post to go upstairs to her closet. Poinsettias were placed around and were the perfect touch. The bigger boys took suitcases upstairs to set them in the hall. And Teller was one. Salty and Felicia would sleep in one of the little girl's rooms and leave their room to Mrs. Thomas to be their guest until Christmas was past.

Felicia had to see Jo's engagement ring and exclaimed over it in great delight. She hugged Jo, and they laughed together. Salty also hugged Jo saying, "I've always wanted a redheaded daughter. Look at all the conniving I've had to do to get one."

Bob heard that and echoed, "Conniving?"

But no one was listening. Or were they ignoring his questioning? How or what had his father "connived"?

While Phillip the chauffeur was again slowly pretending to sip his toddy, more of the family arrived. Cars pulled up in the Saul-cleared area under the winter-naked branches of the elm, and people arrived herding children of various ages up the walks shoveled by the family. The influx of people was amazing.

Bob directed the human traffic and the visitors found signs on the bedroom doors designating who was housed where. It had been efficiently done. It was all so smooth that Phillip realized it was also practiced. The family had done this before. It was one great slumber party.

And it was noisy. Just the laughter was a continuing background. Occasionally there was a shriek or a child's crying to be heard, but there were plenty of adults to see to the cause.

Since they all came home several times during the year, none was a stranger to the inconveniences. No one wanted to be farmed out to other residences, they might miss some of the gossip and they were all reasonably companionable. Bob decided it was mostly that they were all tolerant. He hadn't been home in years. And it was only then he realized that he was truly... home.

Much earlier, Saul, Ben, Jake and Teller had set the tables with Jo and Bob directing and helping.

With all the tables set up in the huge dining room, the family could all be seated. The adults were at one extended table, and Phillip had a place. The middle children were at another table, and the small children were spaced out so that someone could monitor them.

Bob noted Felicia with her elbow on the table, her chin on her fist, listening with that flattering intensity. Salty's head bent as he ate, his attention on a speaker in encouragement. And as always, halfway through the meal, the two moved over to sit with the children, sending two from that table to the adult table.

But Bob mostly noticed Jo. She was charming. She was beautiful. She was perfect. She laughed and listened and soothed little kids and was a part of them all. How could she know so well to do all that when she came from such a cold family?

After the noon meal, there was a rest period shared by the travelers and those who would be in the play. And there was a light supper for all.

Jo, Bob, Felicia and Teller went ahead to the Center.

No one was particularly surprised when Phillip the chauffeur accompanied them. Bob had loaned him a sweater to wear under his coat and a woolen tam to replace the chauffeur's cap. The stretch limo was filled with the older children, who loved the different means of traveling, and the varying Browns all attended the town gathering.

There was no way that they could all sit together. There were so many Browns that the family's men didn't take seats but stood around the outside of the seating area, while the children sat on the floor in front of the stage with other children of the town.

And behind the curtain, the actors could hear the rustling, the whispers and the excitement. It communicated to them and their adrenaline rushed into their bloodstreams.

They took their places as the music began. It was to hush the audience. They played "Santa Claus is Coming to Town." When that was finished, there was applause and then silence. The curtains slowly parted and those on stage could see beyond the footlights to the sparks of light reflected on glasses or jewelry or shiny cloth as people moved to see better or breathed or moved their hands to gesture.

As they quieted, the preacher began, "'Twas the night before Christmas—'" And he paused.

Bob came onstage, and a mouse skittered across in back of him and ducked into a crevice that was just the right size. There was a murmur of appreciation from the audience.

As Papa, Bob was dressed in a white flannel night-shirt that came down to his hairy calves. He wore backless slippers that flopped and a red stocking cap, and he carried a brass candleholder with a lit candle. While the stage was faintly lighted, a spotlight followed Bob as if the illumination was from the candle.

As he moved over the stage, checking the "fire" of colored plastic strips moved upward by a fan, the mice scuttled about, disappearing into holes as Papa's light approached. The kids in the audience giggled.

There was a sleeping "cat" on the sofa who ignored it all. And an alert "dog" lay quietly. He cocked his head at the mouse activity but didn't move. It was cleverly done.

Papa then looked in on the children and finally went to the alcove that contained a bed with Mama already asleep. Papa lifted the covers, sat on the bed, used his toes to remove his slippers, and swung his legs under the covers. He turned to Mama and kissed her to cheers from the men in the audience.

And the Narrator continued. "'—When all through the house, not a creature was stirring, not even a mouse.'"

And a mouse stuck its head out of a hole and peeked around. The audience kids loved it.

The children were snuggled down in their beds, and the sugarplums were dressed in sugary-looking colors as they danced above the sleeping children.

The parents had settled down for their long winter's nap when a clatter sounded on the lawn.

Bob sprang from the bed and went to the window, where he " '—tore open the shutters and threw up the sash.' "

The stagehands showed the moon on the breast of the new fallen snow. They did that marvelously, with pictures and lighting. The audience saw the cleverly shown film of a small sleigh and the tiny reindeer, and they watched " '—as dry leaves that before a wild hurricane fly, when they meet with an obstacle mount to the sky,' " the sleigh and deer appeared to fly closer. They briefly disappeared and suddenly on the roof there were the sounds of reindeer hooves.

And the lights flashed on the prancing and pawing of the eight proud reindeer with clever wire-stiffened and cotton-stuffed antlers. The loaded sleigh was behind the rail of the widow's walk on the far side of the chimney.

It was well done and the audience applauded as they commented in exclamations.

His spotlight stayed on Bob and he turned around as Porter came down the chimney with a bound. Then Porter yiped and hopped out of the fireplace to brush his bottom and it appeared that he'd smothered a singed seat. The audience laughed.

He was dressed all in fur from his head to his foot, and he really was all covered in ashes and soot. " 'He spoke not a word but went straight to his work' " —Porter did the role perfectly.

A little three-year-old mouse came out of her hole and stood bent forward with her little head turned and her little arms cocked and her wrists bent up. She was charming and there were breathless "ohhhhs" softly from the crowd.

As Papa went past and the spotlight hit her, she covered her eyes with her little star hands until the light was past. Then she watched as Bob stopped to witness Santa's work. So she crept forward to wind an arm around Bob's calf and lean against him, watching, too. Bob lay his hand on her head.

Porter examined toys and considered if they were correct for which stocking. He put a stuffed mouse by the sofa "cat" who leaped to the back of the sofa in alarm. The audience loved that.

And mice and sugarplums and children and Mama all crept out of bed to peek from the shadows and to point and pantomime among themselves. After Santa had filled all the stockings and stepped into the chimney to lay a finger to the side of his nose, he gave a nod "'and up the chimney he rose.'" After two tries.

From the roof, someone " 'sprang to the sleigh and to the team gave a whistle.'"

And as the lights went out on the rooftop, the film showed Santa waving as the reindeer leapt away, pulling the sleigh through the night sky, and the audience heard Porter calling, "'Happy Christmas to all and to all a good night!'"

The applause was marvelous.

Everybody had to take a bow and they all did that. There were cheers and laughter and it was wonderful. Mama and Papa stood together to roars of delight, and Bob kissed Jo again.

Teller's antlered head turned to look at them. Bob winked at the boy and Teller smiled.

Then the stage was filled with the carolers. Among them, Bob stood holding Jo's hand. And the mice and sugarplums and children and the antlered deer stood mixed all through the carolers. The house lights came on and there was a rustling as they opened their large-print books, and all the townspeople there sang the Christmas carols.

Children's voices singing are especially touching. Bob thought it took a real believer in Santa to sing that way. And he smiled as they sang "Up on a House-top" —Maybe it was worth fooling the kids.

He looked around at all the faces concentrated on the carols. It was as if the adults had all gone back to their childhoods and were sampling that magic again.

Then he looked at Jo. She was his magic. He squeezed her hand and she lost her place and just smiled up at him. All the other people there vanished and were silent.

Under the voices surrounding them, Bob whispered, "Merry Christmas, Mrs. Brown."

She whispered back, "I still have a while to be Miss Malone."

"For all practical purposes, Mrs. Brown, you are qualified to use my name."

She blushed and her rust eyelashes modestly covered her eyes. "Shame on you, Mr. Brown," she whispered.

"When will you marry me?"

"Tomorrow?"

He was electrified. Then appalled. "I don't have the license."

"Silly." She teased. "I need a little time to get a gown and notify some people about this event."

"It will be an Event. When will this 'event' take place?"

"When do you choose?"

"A week?"

"A *week?*" she gasped.

And someone said, "Sh-h-h."

Jo blushed again. Bob watched, completely unchastened. "Why are you blushing? What are you thinking to make you blush that way? What I'm thinking? Where would you like to go on our honeymoon?"

Jo said, "Sh-h-h."

"I love you, Jo Brown."

And she forgot to sing and just looked up at him.

And in the audience, there were several watchers who had seen the lovers' private exchange of whispers, and their eyes had teared with sentiment as they'd watched.

One was Felicia.

One was an old flame of Bob's youth who sat with her husband, each holding a child. He saw that his wife watched Bob and jealousy stirred anew inside his heart. And he saw the tear trembling on his wife's lashes. But she leaned her shoulder against his and nudged and squirmed it a little so that he knew she wanted him to put his arm around her. He did that with a touch of nostalgic bitterness. But then his wife looked up at him and smiled. He was stunned. She said, "I'm glad you married me." He kissed her temple and then had to spend the rest of the time trying to control his emotions, but a tear leaked from his eye and crept down his cheek. His wife noted that and her heart melted.

And one was a man who loved Jo. Jealousy twisted in him and envy clawed at his heart.

But for the great majority, it was a very satisfying evening.

They had punch that tasted like every other punch for such an occasion, and they had cookies.

And the Browns discovered that their son Creighton had arrived and was standing in back, looking a little alien in that commonly American-looking crowd. His beard was bushy and his eyebrows out of control. He wore a bush jacket and the clothes were worn. He looked like an elegant tramp. They called him Cray.

Felicia didn't have to pretend her greeting, but it was a silent one. She was speechless. She clung to Cray and swallowed and her breath was unsteady, she was so glad to see him again.

When the other Temple residents realized who was the person behind the bush, they slapped his shoulders and exclaimed and questioned. It was just a good thing the play was over or Cray would have stolen the show.

People milled awhile and talked and smiled and wished each other a Merry Christmas, and finally they all went to their homes.

And so did the Browns.

Cray and Bob stood on the porch for a while and just shook their heads and smiled. Cray said, "You got a jewel."

"God, yes. It scares me, she's so perfect."

"You deserve someone who is . . . finally."

"You never took to Debra."

"I saw the dollar signs in her pupils and the bloody claws on the ends of her fingers."

"I didn't until sometime after it was all over. I was really stupid."

"No. You've known too many good people and not enough of the other kind that crawl in this world."

Bob was sober. "You've been dealing with those kind?"

"They're the greedy ones who are ruining this planet."

"People are gradually coming to your way of thinking. Come inside, you're shivering."

"It's cold up here."

Bob laughed. "It has always been cold up here in winter."

"Think of the homeless."

They went silently into the house and they heard Salty saying "—couple of times we thought we might have to stay out in New York until spring!"

But people closed around Cray, and Bob didn't hear why his parents almost had to stay out in New York— until spring?

The yawning little kids were taken to their beds and the older kids got to stay up a little longer. Carols were playing, the tree glittered to call attention to itself and the stacks of presents tempted investigation. But there was always some adult hand that slapped wrists or tweaked an ear and they all said, "No! Not until morning!"

Wine and Christmas cookies were served and the kith and kin all caught up on each other but mostly on Cray. And they drank a special toast to Mike who was in the Persian Gulf.

Then Bob overheard Felicia saying, "Once we almost decided to go on over to London be—"

And Bob frowned. He'd had no idea his parents had been so restless on the east coast. They had been gone for almost a month, but New York wasn't a boring place. If they'd been restless, why hadn't they just come home?

Bob narrowed his eyes and frowned a little. There had been a word Salty had used. An odd word. Contriving? No. Conniving. That was it. Conniving...what?

He saw Jo in the crowd, still in her "kerchief" and long white flannel gown. She looked delicious and she distracted him entirely from consideration of his puzzling parents.

Then some male voice said, "We're all here. Why not now?"

Cray put up a fist and agreed, "Right! We'll have a shivaree!"

Shivaree were for married pe— "What?" Bob asked. "What are you talking about?"

"Let's get the preacher here tonight and get you married. It would save a lot of wear and tear on the family, traveling back here in another week or so. Jo's family is in town. Everybody's here. Let's do it!"

There was a cheer!

"Where would we sleep?" Bob asked.

There were shouts and laughter. "Bob is ready. How about you, Jo?"

"Uh..."

"Great! I'll call your family, and Phillip can go get them in the limo. Okay?"

Across the room Bob and Jo looked at each other in something like shock. Then Bob smiled, and Jo's answering sparkle melted his heart. He called, "Miss Malone, would you do me the honor?"

And she laughed.

There were cheers, and kids crept out of beds to listen and to ask quesitons, or to scold how were they to sleep with all the noise? And they were hushed and explanations were given. So some went back to bed, and the older ones brightened and stayed up. Teller was one.

Salty made a few raspy phone calls and the way was cleared effortlessly. The preacher came with his family and Phillip fetched the Malones. Jo asked Bob's sister, Carol, to be her attendant, and Bob chose his brother, Cray.

The two were married under the mistletoe between the main hall and the living room because everyone could see with them placed there. And it was lovely. Jo was still in her stage costume and Bob pulled his nightshirt from his pants and put his cap on for the most unusual wedding picture anyone there had seen.

The event lengthened the evening considerably and hilariously. With the couple's stage clothing, the witnesses urged Jo's brother John to hold a shotgun on Bob. They'd tape it and send it in to the World's Best Videos and make a fortune. Jo declined. Bob supported that rejection.

So toasts were drunk, the kids were shooed off to bed, sage advice was given, jokes were told, and the preacher and his family left. Phillip was still there, the Malones stayed and the party went on.

Salty kept the attic spotless and there was that ponderous unused four-poster in the attic. Felicia, Georgia, and Carol with some of the other women went to the attic, made up the bed, and put a pot of poinsettias on a table nearby. They blocked off the honeymoon area with elaborate three-sectioned screens.

In one corner of the attic was a small bath the servants had once used but with so many in the household, it was still used and kept spotless. Fresh towels were put there.

The bed-making group went down and announced the honeymoon suite was available, after all! So with great hilarity, too many of them decided to escort the newly wedded couple to their niche and put them into bed.

They finally left them there, reluctantly, and closed the attic door. Bob popped out of bed and bolted the door. Then he came back and smiled almost shyly at his bride. "Did you really want to be hustled into this?"

"Did you?"

"I would have done it weeks ago. I certainly demonstrated that I was interested. How could I be so fortunate to have a family who knew a wavering woman when they saw one and contrived to get—" He stopped.

"What's the matter?"

"'Conniving' was the word Salty used. Josephine Brown, do you suppose we've been manipulated!"

"No!"

"Yes. I believe Salty and Felicia did this to us. Do you know that they probably went off and left us here alone so that with propinquity you'd fall in love with me and have to get married?"

"How shocking."

"Yes. Can you believe that, in this day and age, we are two people who find themselves in an attic, lying in a humongous four-poster, married in our night-clothes, you in your kerchief and I in my cap?"

"You got caught up in the enthusiasm?"

He got up on the high bed. "I sought any excuse to marry you."

"You aren't a victim of circumstances?"

"An eager participant."

"I'm so sleepy, I hope I don't bore you."

"It'll be a change from having you tearing at my clothes, trying to get at my tender body."

"And I *married* you? Good heavens, what happened to clear and practical decisions?"

"Ah, you lucky girl, uh, woman. You have the help of a practical and clear-thinking group to give your life and body direction. They chose me to guide you in this great adventure."

"They've been trying to get rid of you since birth."

"That is true. Do you feel like the sacrificial maiden?"

"No. If you hadn't bolted the door, I would have. I want you compromised so you can't escape me. I told you, you've been my love since I was six."

"A precocious child." He nodded. Then he said thoughtfully, "Do you know that Salty and Felicia were not in the least surprised when they came home and found us engaged?"

Jo considered. "I agree. They didn't seem at all startled. I was. I never really thought we would take this step. That's why I had to sample you while I had the chance."

"If I'd gone on off into the big world out there, what would you have done?"

"Been an old maid. How could I have married any other man? It wouldn't have been fair to him."

"So you love me?"

"Oh, Bob, I love you so much."

"Thank God for that."

"And you? Do you really love me, Bob?"

"So much that with you waffling that way, unsure if this was forever, I seized and encouraged the chance to nail you into a perfect compromise. How can you divorce me now? You consented in front of all those people!'' He laughed dirty. ''I've got you.''

''And...just what do you intend doing about that?''

''Well, at the last minute, Tom handed me some condoms. We'll have a busy night.''

She gasped. ''You trust Tom?''

''Why...no.''

''What'll we do?''

''It just so happens that Cray was smart enough that I directed him to my supply and he smuggled some up here.''

''Which is which?''

''The purple ones are Tom's. Purple for passion, you know.''

''This is a side of Tom I'd never realized.''

''I'm just as glad.''

And they made love. He said she was delicious, and she said he was terrific. They murmured and smoothed their hands on one another possessively and smiled a whole lot. And they cuddled down to sleep.

But in the night, they wakened to find each other and to murmur their pleasure. Bob said, ''See? You're in an honorable marriage. The red hair isn't a curse after all.''

''I only told you that so you could help in my downfall with a clear conscience.''

''Why, Mrs. Brown!'' And he proved to her that it was she who was lascivious; not he, who was just an innocent man.

In the morning, they wandered downstairs rather late for breakfast and found the whole family had been up forever and had already opened their gifts and were getting ready for dinner.

The newlyweds found his parents and Bob said,
"You weren't at all surprised that we were engaged."

The parents smiled a little cautiously.

Bob questioned, "How soon after I called to ask if
I could come home, did you decide on Jo?"

Salty's rasp replied, "Right away."

They didn't even hedge.

Bob nodded thoughtfully, but Jo smiled with the
parents. They all went into the dining room to the tables, where Phillip along with everyone else, stood and
lifted glasses of egg nog. "Merry Christmas!" they
said and smiled at the newlyweds.

"Thank you," Bob replied for the pair.

Then Bob looked at his parents as he took his
bride's hand and lifted it to his lips. And in a husky
voice, he said again, "Thank you."

*   *   *   *   *

This is the season of giving, and Silhouette proudly offers you its sixth annual Christmas collection.

SILHOUETTE

Christmas Stories

1991

Experience the joys of a holiday romance and treasure these heartwarming stories by four award-winning Silhouette authors:

Phyllis Halldorson—"A Memorable Noel"
Peggy Webb—"I Heard the Rabbits Singing"
Naomi Horton—"Dreaming of Angels"
Heather Graham Pozzessere—"The Christmas Bride"

Discover this yuletide celebration—sit back and enjoy Silhouette's Christmas gift of love.

Take 4 bestselling love stories FREE

Plus get a FREE surprise gift!

Angels Everywhere!

Everything's turning up angels at Silhouette. In November, Ann Williams's ANGEL ON MY SHOULDER (IM #408, $3.29) features a heroine who's absolutely heavenly—and we mean that literally! Her name is Cassandra, and once she comes down to earth, her whole picture of life—and love— undergoes a pretty radical change.

Then, in December, it's time for ANGEL FOR HIRE (D #680, $2.79) from Justine Davis. This time it's hero Michael Justice who brings a touch of out-of-this-world magic to the story. Talk about a match made in heaven . . . !

Look for both these spectacular stories wherever you buy books. But look soon—because they're going to be flying off the shelves as if they had wings!

If you can't find these books where you shop, you can order them direct from Silhouette Books by sending your name, address, zip or postal code, along with a check or money order for $3.29 (ANGEL ON MY SHOULDER IM #408), and $2.79 (ANGEL FOR HIRE D #680), for each book ordered (please do not send cash), plus 75¢ postage and handling ($1.00 in Canada), payable to Silhouette Reader Service to:

In the U.S.	In Canada
3010 Walden Ave.	P.O. Box 609
P.O. Box 1396	Fort Erie, Ontario
Buffalo, NY 14269-1396	L2A 5X3

Please specify book title with your order.
Canadian residents add applicable federal and provincial taxes.

ANGEL